Where The Magnolia Trees Bloom

A Novel By Emily Comos

Copyright © 2021 Emily Comos

This is a work of fiction. Names, characters, places, and incidents either are the product of the author's imagination or are used fictitiously. Any resemblance to actual persons, living or dead, events, or locales is entirely coincidental.

All rights reserved. No part of this book may be reproduced in any form on by an electronic or mechanical means, including information storage and retrieval systems, without permission in writing from the publisher, except by a reviewer who may quote brief passages in a review.

ISBN: 9798595416085 (paperback)

TABLE OF CONTENTS

Table of Contents	2
Acknowledgments	3
Chapter One	4
Chapter Two	20
Chapter Three	34
Chapter Four	49
Chapter Five	58
Chapter Six	66
Chapter Seven	86
Chapter Eight	96
Chapter Nine	106
Chapter Ten	118
Chapter Eleven	138
Chapter Twelve	151
Chapter Thirteen	158
Chapter Fourteen	166
Chapter Fifteen	179
Chapter Sixteen	185
Chapter Seventeen	207
Chapter Eighteen	218
Chapter Nineteen	225
Chapter Twenty	237
Chapter Twenty-One	243
Author's Note	259

ACKNOWLEDGMENTS

This book was written when the entire world stood still, plagued by a pandemic and stricken with fear. During those dark and quiet times, I desperately needed an escape, a feeling of hope, something to think about that wasn't my toilet paper stock dwindling or if my parents were going to be okay.

Thank you to my best friend, Rachel, for being the first eyes other than my own to read this and for reading it entirely in one night.

Thank you to my editor, Susan, for spending months perfecting each and every word. You brought this story to life from my initial jumbled thoughts and it would be nothing without your constant support and creativity.

Thank you to my dad, who gifted me with the love of writing.

Thank you to my mom, for believing in me when I didn't believe in myself. And for pushing me to not give up on this.

Lastly, a huge thank you to the year 2020. The stubborn, frustrating, and terrifying moments provided some much needed perspective. It forced me to slow down and put the millions of thoughts in my head onto the paper…finally. Without you, 2020, this book wouldn't exist. Here's to silver linings and better years ahead.

CHAPTER ONE

"Bec, get up! It's our last night in the city of love. You're not spending it on this disgusting old couch binging on peanut M&M's and Matthew McConaughey movies."

I jumped onto her lap and threw the TV remote across the room, then grabbed a handful of her M&M's and shoved them into my mouth before giving her a cocky grin. Bec glared at me like I was the most annoying human on Earth.

"First, you're an idiot. The city of love is Paris." She snatched the bag away from me as I attempted to reach in for more. "Second, Matthew McConaughey, even on a screen, is a better companion for the night than any douchebag you're gonna meet and try to bring home. I'm perfectly content spending my last night here in the comfort of my warm, fuzzy, Minnie Mouse pajamas."

She pushed me off her lap onto the couch, folded her pale, freckle-covered arms across her chest, and gave me the same sarcastic smirk I had just given her.

She clearly needed the next level of convincing so I wasn't giving up. Not tonight.

"The city of love is wherever you want it to be. Try and use that big, smart brain of yours for something other than studying."

Time to get creative.

I hustled over to the window and pulled the blinds back with a flourish, displaying the not-so-glamorous view of the dusty liquor store next door.

"Tonight..." I declared dramatically, "for maybe the last night ever...the city of love is right outside our door, just waiting for us to partake in all its glory. Florence freakin' Italy, baby! Now get your ass off that couch, and let's get ready!"

I let the blinds go and leapt across the room where I knelt at Bec's feet and offered up my best puppy dog eyes.

She looked sharply across the room to Jen, who was standing in the kitchen innocently eating a raspberry yogurt. They locked eyes, and Jen shot me one of her famous "don't involve me in this" looks. Bec let out a defeated sigh.

"Guys!" I shouted, throwing my hands in the air. "You're acting like I'm dragging you to the dentist or something. Come on. It'll be fun!" I could feel two very unmotivated stares aimed at me.

"OK, how about this...I promise not to bring any guys back here." I didn't know if I totally believed this promise, but I was desperate.

Still no response.

"What?! I am capable of such a thing you know."

"Right," Bec finally interjected. "And my legs look like Carrie Underwood's. See, Maggie? I'm using my imagination, just like you asked."

Bec may be incredibly mundane when it comes to nightlife and men, but she sure could be hilarious without even trying.

In my defense, she's making me out to be more scandalous than I actually am. Bec thinks that anything beyond shaking hands with a guy should be saved for marriage. To each her own, but…based on my extremely limited worldly wisdom, life's too short to only shake hands.

"Here." I raised my pinky in the air and held it out in front of her. "Pinky promise not to even look at a guy tonight. No matter how charming and Italian and tan and gorgeous he may be. I, Magnolia Akers, vow to remain celibate this evening in honor of my dear friend and roommate…"

Bec swatted my hand away without completing the sacred pinky promise. Doesn't she know that's considered a sin in some cultures?

"Oh my god. I'll come as long as you just shut up." I flashed her a victorious smile, surprised that she had given in this easily. Normally, I had to bribe them with much more than celibacy. "And go get the remote so I can at least watch my movie while I straighten my hair."

"Yesssssss!" I jumped up and straddled her skinny little body, hugging her around the neck and rocking back and forth. Bec has hated affection ever since we were little, but that has never stopped me from finding new ways to smother her with it. The way she winces every time brings me such joy.

"Get off me, weirdo!"

"I love you, Rebecca Sanders!" I kissed the top of her head

before bounding across the room to fetch the remote.

"Jen, you're coming too." I tossed Bec the remote.

She set down the yogurt and shrugged.

"Well, fighting you on this is clearly not worth it after what I just witnessed. But let's try and keep it low-key tonight because we do have to be up and coherent enough tomorrow to get on an airplane."

"Deal!" I shouted back at her after taking off in a sprint to my room just in case they changed their minds.

When I got to my room, I connected my phone to my bluetooth speaker and clicked shuffle on my "getting ready" Spotify playlist. "Wannabe" by Spice Girls came on first.

Ironic.

I flung open my closet doors and danced my way through the hangers, searching for the perfect outfit that screamed, "Buy me a drink, even though my roommates won't let me take you home."

We'd only been in Italy for a month, and I'd already worn all the clothes I'd packed, some twice. If we weren't being forcibly removed from the country, I definitely would need to go shopping for some extra outfits.

I probably shouldn't be concerned about shopping while a worldwide health crisis is occurring, but I guess everyone handles things differently.

The COVID-19 virus was starting to get really bad in several parts of the world; Italy was considered a "hotspot." The first positive case was a few weeks ago and now, there were thousands more. Our professors and program administrators had been monitoring the situation and had warned us that we might have to go home early. But I never thought they meant this early.

Bec had found us a 4:00pm direct flight from Florence to Detroit. Bec and Jen had both booked their tickets as soon as we found out we had 24 hours to evacuate.

If we're being honest here...I haven't actually booked mine.

I am a huge procrastinator, so it's not like it's out of character or anything for me to put off buying airline tickets, but this is different. Bec and Jen don't know it yet, but...I'm not leaving Italy.

I know that sounds irresponsible and, potentially, dangerous. I mean, I don't even have a place to stay. Our apartments were provided by our program and, if they were sending us all home, I doubt they would just let me hang out indefinitely.

This was one of many details I had not yet considered. I guess I just figured I'd cross those bridges once we got to the airport. What's the worst thing that could happen?

I really didn't want to think about tomorrow though. I was determined to make this the most memorable last night ever. Well, last night for everyone but me.

It was definitely going to be a bit difficult given the two stodgy ladies in the living room whom I happened to call my best friends, but I was always up for a challenge.

Especially when alcohol was involved.

I settled on a pair of white jeans with a snakeskin crop top, black heels, and medium-sized black hoops. I looked myself up and down in the mirror hanging on the back of my bedroom door and gave myself a nod of approval.

Not to toot my own horn, but I looked pretty damn good.

I sat down at my desk and brushed my obnoxiously long hair. I'd been trying to grow it out for a while now, but it was currently stuck in this annoying length where it just made me hot all the time. I'd debated cutting it myself a handful of times, but I knew my stylist back home would shun me for messing with her masterpiece.

My hair has been every color you can imagine. I fully believe hair is supposed to change with not only the seasons but also with your moods and experiences.

Bad break up? *Jet black.*

Summer on the lake? *Platinum blonde.*

Overall rebellion and "take over the world" phase? *Purple. Streaks.*

For my current study abroad phase, I decided on probably the most subtle color I'd had in a while: my natural light brown with dirty blonde highlights in the front. I might stick with this look for a while, you know, try to look like an adult or whatever.

Late February in Florence was much more tolerable than in Michigan, but it still got kind of chilly at night, so I grabbed a black leather jacket before heading back out into the living room.

Bec and Jen were pouring wine into small plastic cups. I grinned at them with a look of sheer pride.

"Getting a head start, are we, ladies?"

I was going to grab another cup from the stack on the counter but decided to just take a swig from the bottle instead. Quicker and more efficient, if you ask me.

"We're just trying to save some money by hopefully buying fewer drinks tonight. Not all of us can snap our fingers and get every Joe,

Jim, and Jared in the bar to pay for our tabs."

"I'll take that as a compliment." I took another long swig of the sweet rosé. "But you guys know I would never go for a Joe...*again*." I winked and did a small twirl.

"Are you guys almost ready? I found where we're going." I pulled out my phone. "It's called Silk, and it's low-key just like you wanted. I read about it on some travel blogger's Instagram. She said it's a 'hidden gem'." I turned my phone to show them the photos of the entrance I'd found.

"Can't be that hidden if she's posting about it on Instagram." Bec took a dainty sip of wine, her forehead slightly furrowed.

"Guess we'll find out." I playfully smacked Bec's tiny butt, barely dodging her return swipe.

Bec had, as usual, opted for a more conservative outfit: a pair of skinny jeans and a white, short-sleeved, collared blouse with black and white low-top converse sneakers.

Jen looked a little more sleek with a high pony, long yellow chandelier earrings dangling above her shoulders, a simple black sleeveless shift dress that fell right above her knees, and black leather sandals. If you lined up the three of us, I would definitely look a bit overdressed, but that wasn't hard to do with these two.

We headed downstairs and waited on the sidewalk for a few minutes until an empty cab came by. Bec assertively flagged it down. The drive to Silk was only 10 minutes, and Bec and Jen were somehow buzzed from the wine, which made the ride slightly more entertaining.

Jen asked the driver to roll down her window so she could hang her head out like a dog, and Bec insisted on putting extra lipstick on me, even though she smeared it with every pothole we hit. The second-hand embarrassment was mildly nauseating. To top it off, when we arrived, Bec, being Bec, thanked the driver for "his service."

Deep breath Mags, the alcohol is only a few steps away.

At least we'd gotten there before 10pm, which was when the "ladies' night" special ended and the cover charge increased from 10 to 20 euros per person. We glided in swiftly past the long line of guys waiting anxiously.

The club wasn't exactly as chill as "Wanderlust Willa" had made it out to be. There were three stories and about 5 different bars all lit up with neon lights and dancers on tall platforms wearing barely anything.

Maybe I read the blog post wrong?

Oops.

I could see the panic on Bec's face as she slowly looked around, taking it all in. I decided intervention in the form of alcohol was necessary…ASAP.

"Shots! On me!" I threw my arms up, trying to block Bec's view of the dancers.

Bec and Jen looked at each other immediately, like they needed each others' approval before agreeing.

"Just one! And clear liquor only!" Bec shouted into my ear, attempting to be heard above the pulsing music.

We made our way to the nearest bar and nestled into a small opening at the end. I waved my hand to get the bartender's attention, but it took about three tries for him to notice me amidst the other dozen screaming girls. Being a bartender must make you feel really wanted.

"Three shots of vodka, please." I held up 3 fingers and spoke loud and clear, hoping he'd understand me. I didn't usually try to speak in Italian unless I absolutely had to. Most times, I just end up unintentionally offending someone or humiliating myself in the process.

"Ne avremo quattro per favore!" An unfamiliar voice boomed behind me.

I couldn't translate his entire sentence, but I definitely heard, "Four, please."

I twisted to get a glimpse of the person who apparently wanted to join our party. An overwhelmingly tall man was pushing his way past Bec and Jen to get next to me at the bar. Bec recoiled dramatically and gasped as if someone had just slapped her.

He rested his elbows on the bar and looked over at me casually, like we'd known each other for years. I was pretty used to guys offering to buy me drinks, but this one was pushier than usual. Where did he even come from?

I snapped my gaze back to the bartender, still standing in front of us and waiting impatiently.

"Three is fine. Thanks." The bartender rolled his eyes before turning away to pour our shots.

"More of a beer guy anyway." The gentleman standing obnoxiously close to me shrugged smugly. His breath heated up the side of my face; I got a whiff of vodka and peppermint.

He looked very Italian with rich brown curly hair, a deep tan, and a thin stubble that perfectly framed his extremely handsome face. I was caught off guard, however, by how amazing his English was. His accent was thick but even with the music pounding, I could understand him perfectly.

"Do you need help with something?"

That might've been slightly rude of me, but I could feel Bec observing my every move, and I wasn't in the mood to deal with any drama.

"Well...since you wouldn't let me get a shot with you, I guess I'll settle for help learning your name."

Oh, here we go.

"Good one." I shifted my gaze away from him, attempting to demonstrate my lack of interest. "I'll give that a...7 for creativity." I smiled but kept my eyes focused forward, refusing to look at him.

"7/10? That's 70%, so I passed, right?"

I laughed under my breath, trying not to give him the satisfaction of thinking he's charming. Guys that look like this definitely don't need to be reminded.

The bartender returned with our shots. I had my credit card out and ready so I wouldn't annoy him any further. When he set our drinks down, I held out my card.

Before I could even react, Mr. Italy next to me had snatched the card out of my hand, dropped it in my purse, and given the bartender his card instead. The assertiveness was slightly attractive but, once again, a bit much.

"Why did he just buy our drinks, Maggie? What did you say to him?" Bec whispered not-so-subtly into my ear.

"I bought your drinks because your friend here is the most stunning girl I've ever seen. And I really thought the world was going to end if I didn't buy her that drink."

My jaw began to drop as I watched him interact so effortlessly with Bec. She's not easy to make speechless, but even she hesitated for a moment out of pure shock. This man knew what he was doing.

"Well, she is my friend." Bec finally interjected. "And yes, she is stunning. But you're a bit pushy. And she's unavailable tonight. So thank you for the drinks sir, but we will be on our way now." Bec flipped her hair sassily. He cocked his head slightly, clearly both taken aback and amused by her bluntness.

Bec took one shot glass and passed it to Jen before grabbing the other two along with my arm. As she yanked me away from the bar, I looked over my shoulder and mouthed, "thank you" to him. He tipped his head, and a broad smile overtook his chiseled face.

I followed them to the edge of the dance floor.

"Okay, we've escaped from the evil bar man, can we stop now, please?"

Bec stopped and handed me one of the shot glasses. She raised her glass with an innocent smile, as if she hadn't just royally cock-blocked me.

"He may have been physically attractive, Maggie. But he didn't seem to understand personal space and he clearly had aggression issues. I was doing you a favor."

She threw back her shot and shuddered violently. I wanted to argue with her, but I decided to let it go. I had made a promise, after all, and I wasn't in the mood to fight.

The three of us held hands and danced for a half-hour or so before needing a break from the sweat and the noise and the crowd. Bec and Jen went to find the bathroom while I made it my mission to get some fresh air.

I fought my way to the front entrance and signaled to the bouncer that I just needed to go out for a second. He clearly didn't understand me at all but waved me out anyway. I passed him and smiled sweetly, hoping he'd remember and let me back in.

I made my way to a small roped off section that hugged the side of the building.

It felt fantastic to be alone in the cool night air. I exhaled deeply and glance to my right, then to my left, taking in all the different personalities in the groups huddled near me.

I couldn't understand any of their conversations, but the fresh air was already helping cure to cure my headache, so I decided to stay put for a while.

Just as I was finishing enjoying the much-needed break outside, I nearly choked on a gigantic cloud of cigarette smoke blown in my direction. I turned angrily, ready to scold the rude human who just ruined my $80 perfume, when I realized just who the culprit was.

He didn't see me at first so I could probably have slipped back inside without him noticing. Which I absolutely should have done, but I just couldn't help myself...

I took a step closer as he blew another huge smoke cloud up into the air.

Gross.

But still hot.

"Nasty habit you've got there. Gotta take a couple points off your score for that."

He immediately whipped around and nearly choked on his own smoke.

"I'm thinking you're down to a 5 now."

He looked me up and down slowly. I felt uncomfortable, but I also weirdly liked it. He took yet another deep drag and exhaled a perfectly cocky smoke ring that eventually disappeared over my head.

"You know I don't actually smoke, right?" He pulled the cigarette out of his mouth and waved it delicately in front of me.

I laughed, loudly this time. "So I'm hallucinating that disgusting thing that was just between your lips?"

"Why were you looking at my lips?" He was now staring at my lips as well. I felt my cheeks flush and quickly averted my eyes to absolutely anything else.

"You're not hallucinating. But...it's only there so pretty girls like you will come up and tell me that smoking is bad for me. That I should quit. What would you have said if I hadn't had this?" He began to place it back between his lips.

Damn it, he's good.

Really good.

"Well played." I took the cigarette from his mouth, threw it on the ground between us, and crushed it with my heel. "But I would've come over here regardless. If for no other reason than to apologize for my...over-protective friend."

"Ah yes, tiniest bodyguard I've ever seen. But still scary, I'll give her that."

"She's just a bit paranoid. Watches too much TV, you know? But someone in the group has to be the one, so we don't end up on the morning news."

He took another step closer to me. "And I'm assuming that's never been your role."

I was starting to feel a bit dizzy, but I couldn't tell if it was from the alcohol or him. Or both. I tried to keep my cool but could feel it wasn't working.

"No, I have a different role." I stepped closer now, leaving barely any space between us. "I'm the fun one."

He smirked as he stared down at me, and I could tell at that exact moment that he was trouble.

The best kind of trouble.

"It's a good thing I like fun."

I really needed to pull back and stop flirting immediately or I was going to get myself into trouble, and not the sexy, Italian kind.

He placed his hand on my shoulder, paused, and continued to look at me. It seemed like he was waiting for me to signal my consent.

No man, and I mean not a single one, has ever hesitated like that.

Finding a man asking for consent to be this attractive? Yeah, the expectation bar was literally on the floor. But it did catch me off guard and only made me more into him.

I smiled, welcoming the warmth of his hand now pressing

against my upper back. He slowly slid down the back of my leather jacket and I shivered, but not because I was cold. I didn't usually let strangers touch me this quickly, but he was intoxicating. And I was just tipsy enough to not feel any apprehension. With his other hand, he brushed a stray wisp of hair off my cheek and then began to lean in.

As I closed my eyes in anticipation, I heard a frustratingly familiar voice approaching.

"Get off of her right now, you creep!" Bec was standing behind us with her hands on her hips. Jen stood next to her looking somewhat embarrassed, but I knew she'd never admit it.

"Bec, relax! We were just talking. He's fine."

"He is certainly not fine, Maggie. You are drunk, and he was taking advantage of you. I saw it with my own eyes. We are leaving. Now!"

She stormed off and, to no one's surprise, Jen followed close behind like a lost puppy. She snuck a quick sympathetic look back at me as she exited the roped-off section.

We watched them leave for a few seconds with our mouths open. Then, we looked back at each other and burst out laughing.

He reached his hand out slowly, and I looked up at him.

"It's nice to meet you, Maggie. I'm August."

I realized I hadn't even told him my name, and I was just about to let him kiss me. God, I have a serious weakness for these Italian men. I shook his hand and smiled.

"Nice to meet you as well, August...I'm so sorry, but I have to go."

He nodded and carefully released my hand, like he was afraid to hurt me. I wanted to say more, do more, just be with him more, but not even this man was worth getting into a fight with Bec. If I broke my promise tonight, she would never let me hear the end of it.

I pulled myself away from him and started walking toward Bec and Jen who were now standing at the entrance. Bec looked extremely pissed and was clearly complaining about me to Jen. I paused and turned around to take one last look at August.

He was in the same spot, still watching me, a noticeable grin on his face.

I can't remember the last time I felt this conflicted. There was something different about this guy. Something that made me want to desperately break all the rules.

It took every last shred of willpower I had to force myself to turn around and walk toward the entrance but I finally pulled myself away.

This was ultimately why I wanted to stay in Italy. No, not specifically for him, I only just met the guy after all. But these were the kind of people who I wanted to continue meeting. The moments I wanted to experience and the risks I wanted to take, without the constant judgement following my every move.

Tomorrow, when I'm officially on my own, it's time for a new chapter.

CHAPTER TWO

Florence International Airport was insane the next afternoon. There were floods of tourists, all trying to catch the last few flights back to wherever. Some were wearing medical masks, which was slightly worrisome. It really was beginning to look like a scene from an end of the world movie. The three of us stood in the lobby.

"Guys, listen. I promise I will be fine. Please just go." I hoped I sounded more confident than I felt.

Obviously, I hadn't given much thought about how this would go or even where I would stay, but I just knew that I couldn't go home.

My father, Gary, had recently moved to a smaller condo because it was just him now. It would be very tight if I chose to stay there with him, and privacy would be non-existent. The only benefit of living with mom and her new husband, Roger, would be their gigantic house and pool. However, neither option was even slightly intriguing.

When my parents got divorced, I was only a freshman in high school. I think I was too young to really grasp all the complications of a divorce. To me, it just felt like double the holidays and dad constantly buying the wrong shampoo for me.

To my knowledge, the main causes of their split were my mom's lack of financial responsibility and drinking too much, too often.. Ever since I was little, she couldn't keep a steady job. I think she was mostly fired for being late. She couldn't get up in the morning because she was always hungover. But not having a job didn't stop her from charging up my dad's credit cards. She was literally addicted to shopping, clothes mostly. Then, after my dad cut up her cards, she started milking off Gram, her mom, which also ended very poorly.

My dad was always kind and caring, too much so sometimes. In my eyes, he could do no wrong. Therefore, I only had her to blame for ripping our family apart. I didn't want to see her so I spent most of my time at my dad's. Then, eventually, my dad got full custody of me for the last two years of high school. Now, I really only see my mom on holidays and even that's too much for me, especially now that Mr. "Bring me a beer" is always in attendance.

My mom seemed to meet Roger alarmingly quickly after she and my dad split, like so quickly that I really wondered if they had gotten together while my parents were still married. I'm not sure what she sees in him besides his money. Or...maybe that's all she sees, and that's enough for her. My mom is so preoccupied with making sure Roger constantly has a beer in his hand that she wouldn't even notice if I came home from Italy or not.

My dad would definitely be more concerned, but he was easier to convince. I think he still felt guilty about the divorce even though it wasn't his fault at all. He was super understanding when it came to my fuck-ups; hopefully this decision wouldn't be placed in that category.

I waited until the literal moment we got to the airport to tell Bec and Jen about my decision because, honestly, I didn't want to deal with all the shit I knew they were going to give me. Traveling in general sends them into a spiral of worrying. So, then, if you add in a deadly virus and leaving your best friend behind in a foreign country, you end up with tears and hyperventilating.

"Maggie, where will you go? They gave us specific orders to get back home as quickly as we possibly could, and you're talking about doing the exact opposite! I don't think you're taking this seriously enough!"

Bec was waving her hands frantically as she made each point, her vibrant red curls swinging back and forth. I think she thought this would convey her point better, but she just looked like she was trying to swat a fly. If the people passing us hadn't been so focused on catching their flights, she would've been causing a much bigger scene.

As I'm sure you've noticed by now, Bec is the planner of our group. She's also relentless in her pursuit of control, as you could clearly see from her unrestrained encounters with August last night.

She's been like this ever since we both joined student council in 5th grade. Someone needed to take charge of planning every excruciating detail of every excruciating moment of the Halloween dance, and I couldn't have cared less about stuff like that. I just wanted us to look badass in our matching Powerpuff Girl costumes.

I knew traveling out of the country for an entire semester would be difficult with her, but I also knew it'd be barely any work for me because she'd have our every move calculated and scheduled down to the minute. Bec's type-A personality was both a blessing and a curse.

Jen is slightly less anxiety-ridden than Bec, but not by much. I actually met Jen first. We were table partners in Mrs. Rogers' third grade class. She has always been ridiculously smart and the sweetest girl you'll ever meet. She's always the first to ask what's wrong and offer you a helping hand. When my parents got divorced, Jen brought me homemade desserts every single night for a week. Frankly, the girl just has no backbone, especially when Bec is involved.

Bec says "jump," and Jen says, "How high? What should I do next?"

Both Jen and I had basically just gotten used to accepting whatever Bec had planned for us. We always knew that the plan was carefully crafted to be: safe; well-thought-out; and balanced with respect to each of our interests (Bec's "big three" for planning anything). But this time was different.

I couldn't just go along with the plan this time because that meant I would have to go back to the boring life I was trying to escape by coming to Italy in the first place.

"Hotels are still open, Bec. And I can probably still get an AirBnB if I try right now. You know they're just trying to scare us with the 24-hour travel restriction. If it really were that bad, we wouldn't even be allowed to get on a plane or go home." I didn't actually know if that was true, but, hopefully, it sounded convincing enough to get Bec and Jen on that damn plane.

They looked at each other, a healthy combination of doubt and fear telepathically traveling between the two of them.

"What about school? How are you going to finish the semester from here?"

"Bec, we don't even know what school is going to look like with this virus...they could cancel classes for the semester if it gets really bad. Or maybe switch everything to online. Whatever happens, I'll figure it out."

I think this was the point when they realized that changing my mind was impossible. I'd always been stubborn. When I decided on something, it was ridiculously hard to convince me otherwise.

They both shook their heads in defeat and grabbed the handles to their rolling suitcases.

"You better be so fucking careful, Mag. Like more careful than me and Jen put together, and that's more careful than you've ever been in your entire life."

I could've been insulted by this, but she wasn't wrong. I was pretty notorious for being the exact opposite of careful. Life gets boring when you always followed the rules. I think I read that in a Dr. Seuss book or something, but it really was true.

I nodded somberly, maintaining a super serious expression and willing them to leave. Bec suddenly took a step much closer to me; her eyes met mine like she was staring into my soul.

"Get to a hotel, and don't leave. Like, don't even go grocery shopping. Just order takeout or something. This is serious, Maggie. I can feel it. I don't have a good feeling about leaving you here, but I know I can't convince you to leave. I want you to be happy, but I also need you to be alive and healthy. So please, if you listen to just one thing I say, let it be this. Just...stay...inside. Wait for this to all blow over. Don't do anything crazy." She took a deep breath.

"We love you, and we're going to miss you."

Before I could even respond, they were both hugging me tightly. To my surprise, my eyes filled with tears. As much as these girls drove me crazy, I loved them both more than life itself.

After breaking the world record for the longest hug ever, they headed toward the security line without saying another word. Once they got in line, they both turned and waved, their faces lined with worry. I smiled reassuringly and waved back, happy to finally be alone.

Bec was right, though. I needed to figure out a place to stay before everything shut down. I began to worry, for the first time, that this whole situation actually might be more complicated than I was making it out to be in my head. But there was no turning back now; I had to focus and figure out a game plan.

I needed to find a hotel and, preferably, one that wouldn't cost me my entire savings account.

I called probably a dozen; they either didn't answer or their lines were busy.

Ok, let's not panic.

I sighed and put my phone down. It vibrated, and I grabbed it, expecting it to be one of the hotels returning my call. Instead, a message from Jen appeared.

We're at the gate now. Bec doesn't know I'm sending you this but I'm proud of you. It takes guts to do what you're doing. I can't wait to hear about your adventure. Love you!

I smiled and sent back three red heart emojis. Like I said, sweetest girl ever. I felt a tiny wave of hope flutter through me knowing that at least one person was on board with my crazy plan.

Just as I was about to call yet another hotel, a middle-aged woman abruptly plopped down next to me on the bench, uncomfortably close for my liking. Europeans didn't believe in personal space.

She was clearly unhappy with whoever was on the other end of the phone call. She spoke English effortlessly.

"Yes, well, I'm sure you understand that we were counting on a May first launch like we agreed on."

I snuck a look at her. As she listened to his response, she rolled her eyes and then took a deep breath.

"Yes, of course I'm aware of the Covid-19 virus, but that doesn't explain why you chose to cancel our meeting. And why you chose to do so two hours before my flight. And, unless you have a crystal ball, you don't know what the market will be like this summer. People will probably drink more wine if this thing gets worse."

She had frizzy, untamed, shoulder-length black hair that was loosely held together by a large gold and white polka dot barrette. Her lean frame swam in the long black sundress she wore.

She wasn't taking any shit from the person on the other end of the phone call -- most likely a man -- and I was loving it.

She ended the call after taking a slow breath in and out.

"I'm very disappointed with your decision. And I'm sure Leone will be as well." I'm going to go now. Goodbye." She threw her phone into the bag on the floor.

"This virus is going to give me gray hair, and, lord help me, I refuse to leave this world with gray hair." She didn't look at me when she spoke, but there wasn't anyone else around that she could have been speaking to.

I laughed, and she joined me. She looked at me, shaking her head -- two strangers, sitting together on a bench amidst a mad rush of people, just sharing a laugh. It was refreshing and much needed right now.

"He kinda seemed like a jerk."

"He doesn't think now is the best time to be "branching out." She used her fingers to create air quotes.

"Branching what out?" I asked without hesitation, turning my body to face her. It was probably way too nosy of me, but I was weirdly curious about this feisty woman.

"My husband and I run a vineyard. We've been trying for years to get our wines to the US market. And last year, we finally found an investor who seemed like he was...on the same page with us, and we came up with a really solid...agreement, and we were supposed to have our wines in U.S. stores this summer. Looks like the virus had other plans for us, though."

"Wow, you own a vineyard? That's amazing. Is it near here?"

Are you kidding me?

"Yes, we do. It's out in the country, about an hour from here."

I nodded, trying to hide my excitement. This stranger was living my ideal life: owning a dreamy Italian vineyard in the country like she was the main character in a foreign movie.

"I'm so sorry about your investor. I hope it all works out for you and your husband."

"God, I hope so too. We have three kids, one pursuing a very expensive college education and two who are equally expensive in their own ways."

She checked her watch. "I was supposed to fly out at 6:00 to make some final decisions on the packaging and labels. He told me not to board the plane and that our wine wasn't hitting U.S. shelves anytime soon."

"I'm so sorry. I know what it's like to have everything change so suddenly, but I still can't imagine what you're going through."

She looked at me with a warm smile. "Thank you. I appreciate that. Once this whole thing blows over, I'm sure we'll get back on our feet, and, hopefully, our wines will make it to America someday. You'll have to try them sometime when you get back home and let me know what you think." She winked at me, knowing very clearly that I was a tourist.

"I will be sure to do that."

There was about a ten-second pause during which I debated whether or not I should tell her about my situation.

I'm not going back right now, actually. My friends are on the last flight to the US tonight, but I'm planning on staying here to quarantine. Much better food than the American Midwest."

Her face dropped. "Your friends left you here? Alone?"

"Well, they didn't exactly leave me. I sort of...forced them to go without me. I absolutely love it here, and I refuse to let my trip be cut short over this.

"Honey..." She paused and took a deep breath. "I fear this is much, much worse than you think it is. I've never seen our country like this. I've never seen the world like this. And I've seen some pretty messed up stuff in my lifetime." I could hear the genuine concern in her voice, which caused me to begin to worry as well. "You should've gone home with your friends. It's not safe for you to be here all alone."

"Oh, I'll be okay. I have some money saved up for emergencies, and I have experience traveling alone." This was a lie. I'd never traveled anywhere without family or friends. But she was a mother, and I knew that she'd naturally worry, so I tried to soothe her concern.

Like, come on. How hard could this be? I've seen "Eat, Pray, Love" at least a dozen times.

"Where will you even stay? I doubt hotels or bed and breakfasts are going to stay open much longer. Everything in the city is shutting down. It's going to be like the apocalypse here."

An unwelcome wave of doubt fluttered through me.

"I appreciate your concern...I really do. But I'll be fine." I'm going to take a taxi back to Florence and wander around until I find a hotel that's still open. All I have is this suitcase and my backpack, so I can walk for a while." My total lack of planning sounded really dumb when said out loud.

She shook her head aggressively. "Nonsense. You're what...19? 20 years old? I can't send you out there knowing you'll be alone with nowhere to go. I refuse to have that bad karma on my conscience. It's just not safe. Listen, this is going to sound crazy, but...how about you come stay with us...on the vineyard. We have an extra bed for you and plenty of space."

I had to physically fight my jaw from dropping onto the floor. This stranger was not actually inviting me to stay at her Italian vineyard, was she?

I'd heard stories from friends who'd studied abroad about how generous people in foreign countries were. They'd meet people at a bar who would end up offering to host them for the entire weekend.

I thought for a brief moment about how furious Bec would be that I was even considering such an insane proposal. But the fact was...this woman was right. I had nowhere to go and, as much as I hated to admit it, I truly had no clue how bad this virus could get. And hey, what's the worst that could happen? I might even get some free wine out of it if I played my cards right.

She looked at me intently, then took my hand in hers and squeezed it gently.

"Just stay for a few nights until you get a better plan in place. Or stay until you decide to go back home. It doesn't matter to me how long you stay, as long as you're safe."

I knew she was right. And, call me naive, but I had a really strong feeling that this woman was completely harmless.

"You're sure I wouldn't be imposing? I really would be okay on my own."

"Of course not. You know what? We could actually really use your help preparing for the summer season. Trust me. There are plenty of projects to keep you busy. I can't pay you, but I can offer you home-cooked meals, a cozy bed, and a crazy bunch of kids to hang out with. How's that for a tempting offer?"

I felt better knowing that I could work at the vineyard. I really didn't want to be too much of an inconvenience.

There was no way in hell I was turning this down.

I took a deep breath and smiled at her. "I accept your offer, and I'd be more than happy to help with whatever projects or work you have for me. I'm very grateful for your hospitality; you're really too kind...you literally just met me."

"Not at all." She stood up in one fluid movement and reached her hand out to help me up. "A very long time ago, I traveled abroad as well, and I occasionally found myself in situations not unlike yours. Many kind and gracious people helped me along my journeys, so I'm simply repaying the favor. We're not so different, you know."

I smiled, thinking to myself how fun and wild she must've been back in her younger days.

"I should probably know the name of my new employee." She leaned over and grabbed the strap of my backpack and flung it over her shoulder.

"It's Maggie." I reached my hand out to shake hers. "So nice to meet you."

"Maggie, I'm Fran, and the pleasure is all mine."

I figured I should maybe call my parents to let them know what was going on. Not that I necessarily cared what they had to say about it.

Our family was never all that close. Even before my parents got divorced, I spent most of my childhood at my Gram's house. She lived right down the street from us, and I would walk there nearly every day after school. She would have these amazing, fresh-baked, double chocolate chip cookies ready when I got there. And she always made time to help me with my homework, unlike my mom who was usually a glass or two into the wine by the time I got home. I don't even think she noticed I was gone half the time.

Gram always knew what was really going on with me — good or bad. And she would never tell me what to do. She would just listen and then say, "I know you will figure this out. Listen to your gut."

She definitely would have encouraged me to stay here in Italy. She told the best stories about when she was young. One time, she got into an elevator at a hotel in London, and Paul McCartney was casually standing in there. She couldn't think of anything to say. He got off on the next floor, and, as the doors closed, she yelled, "I love you, Paul!"

I'm doing this, taking this risk, for Gram. I did listen to my gut, and it told me to trust this stranger. She would be proud of me for saying yes to life and the unique opportunities that are presented to us when we least expect it. I just wish she was still here so I could share all this with her.

I called my mom first, and she didn't answer. Probably rubbing Roger's nasty feet or something equally patriarchal.

Dad didn't pick up either. Was he dealing with Sam and/or

Derek, my two older brothers? Dad always seemed to be the one picking up the slack with those two. I had no doubt they would both be heading back to quarantine with one of our parents. They would do anything for free food, laundry, and ESPN.

I left a message on my dad's voicemail explaining that I wouldn't be coming home just yet but that I was perfectly safe and had a place to stay. I tried to include some details about it being a work opportunity to satisfy his concerns and help me avoid answering a million questions when he called back.

I hung up and jogged back over to Fran who was scrolling through her phone, our luggage at her feet.

"All set? Parents give you the ok?"

"All set," I lied. "We're good to go." Truthfully, it didn't really matter what my parents had said or not said at this point. I had made my decision, and, in 12 hours, I wouldn't be allowed to go home even if I wanted to.

As we drove out of the airport parking lot, Fran turned on the radio.

"Here we go." Fran looked over at me and grinned.

I smiled back at her. "I'm ready."

CHAPTER THREE

Surprisingly, Fran didn't talk as much as I thought she would on the drive back. She asked a few questions about my life and family, then told me I'd be sharing a room with her youngest daughter, Bel. I think she could tell I was exhausted when I rested my head against the window. She turned up the radio and hummed along.

I had so many questions about the vineyard and her family, but my mind was racing in about a hundred different directions. I was thinking about my family, Bec and Jen, all the phone calls I had to make, the virus...but strangely, most of my thoughts revolved around August.

He would not leave my brain. I wish I would've gotten his phone number or social media or something. I didn't even know his last name. If Bec hadn't been rushing me, I may have been able to somehow see him again. I guess everything happens for a reason, even if that reason is your paranoid best friend.

When we arrived, we pulled down a long gravel driveway. As I stepped out of Fran's Jeep, I could hear crickets chirping. Every so often, a bullfrog croaked loudly. I took a deep breath of the fresh country air and let my eyes close for a moment in preparation for whatever was to come.

It was already pretty dark so I couldn't make out the details of the house, but I could tell it was enormous. It made my dad's house look like a little tiki hut.

I struggled to roll my suitcase across the gravel as I followed Fran. We came in through a side door. The kitchen was quiet and dim. I was pretty relieved that there wasn't a large welcoming committee to greet me.

Fran gave me a brief tour, showing me where the snacks and drinks were, as well as extra towels and linens. She told me to help myself to anything and everything, including the wine she pointed to above the refrigerator. She gave me a tiny wink and just continued with the tour, so I couldn't exactly tell if she was being serious, but I hoped she was because I was thinking that I could really use a glass of wine.

We ended up at Bel's room, which was to be my room as well. Remnants of a birthday celebration were scattered about: streamers, a large banner, and two giant, semi-deflated, pink mylar balloons in the shape of a one and a six.

The guest bed was nicely made up with a simple white comforter and white pillows and was in direct contrast to Bel's, which was adorned with a bright pink polka dot comforter, faux fur blanket, and about 8 pillows, all different shades of pink and purple.

"Bel, this is Maggie. She's going to be staying with us for a bit. She was a student in Florence, but her school's housing complex is closing because of the virus."

"So, she's American?" Bel asked Fran abruptly. Dramatically lifting her eyes from my feet to the top of my head, she slowly set her phone down and made direct eye contact with me.

"Yes, Bel. Now, be nice." Fran walked over to Bel and planted a big kiss on the top of her head before motioning for me to make myself comfortable on the other bed. Bel continued to stare at me blankly.

"Hi Bel. It's nice to meet you, and um...thanks for sharing your room. I really appreciate it. Oh, and happy belated." I gestured toward the decorations.

She was surveying me now, trying to figure me out. "Thanks, and no problem. I've always wanted a sister. But don't go touching my stuff; I don't know if I can trust you yet." She grinned at me slyly. I didn't feel so uncomfortable anymore. I could tell she was just the right amount of sassy. I could also tell we were going to get along just fine.

"Maggie, you must be hungry. How about I heat up some of Leone's famous spinach lasagna for you?"

I suddenly realized that I was absolutely starving. "I don't want to impose."

"Don't be silly. It'll just take a minute. I'm going to have some too. We both missed dinner!"

I nodded to accept her offer.

"Get yourself settled in and meet me in the kitchen whenever you're ready." Fran smiled as she left Bel's room.

We engaged in super brief small talk as I started to unpack a few things from my bag. Once the conversation slowed, I grabbed my pajamas and toiletry bag, then asked Bel where the bathroom was. She pointed. "All the way down the hall."

Bel's room was the first one at the top of the stairs so I had to pass quite a few other rooms to get to the bathroom that all the kids shared. All the doors were closed. Fran and Leone's room was on the first floor, and they had their own bathroom, which was more than a slight relief. I really needed to freshen up if I was going to meet any other family members tonight.

The bathroom door was closed as well. I knocked, and a deep, male voice replied, "Can you just give me a second?" I smoothed out my frizzy airport hair and breathed into my hand to see how putrid my breath was.

The tall male exited the bathroom with only a white bath towel wrapped around his waist. He turned and saw me waiting in the hall.

"Maggie!?"

Holy shit.

I blinked aggressively a few times.

"August?"

"Oh my god." We said this at the same exact time.

Neither of us could move from the shock.

"What the hell are you doing here? How are you here? What is happening right now?" He was rambling, and he sounded quite alarmed. Did he think I followed him home from the bar and broke into his house or something?

"I sort of met your mom, well, I'm assuming Fran is your mom, at the airport, and she…invited me to like stay with you guys."

His eyes lit up and a smile slowly grew on his face as he shifted from confused to excited. I could see the tension release from his broad, bare shoulders.

"Leone mentioned at dinner that mom was bringing a student home from the airport, but I'm…just…I can't believe it's you. That you're here. This shit just doesn't happen."

It suddenly struck me that this magnificent, sexy man was standing in front of me practically naked. I was really trying not to let my eyes drift too much from his face. How is this happening right now?

"I…I'm…completely at a loss for words…but I'm happy to see you again."

He looked up and down my body with eyes so intense that they lit all the butterflies in my stomach on fire. He grinned devilishly.

"Oh…I am happy to see you too. You said you were the fun one…this is going to be fun, Ms. Maggie." The way he said "fun" made me blush.

His curls were still wet, and he smelled like fresh pine. Dozens of tiny freckles were sprinkled across his olive cheeks, and when he smiled, he had only one tiny dimple on his right cheek. His dark brown eyes seemed to go right through me. There were still a few droplets of water on his sculpted, hairless chest.

"Well, welcome to the family, Maggie. It's a bit crazy at times, but I think you'll have a good time while you're here. I plan to make sure of it."

God, I really wish I would've popped in a mint.

"Thank you, August." I smiled up at him casually.

He nodded. "And hey, if you ever need anything, just knock on your wall. My bed's on the other side. So if you're ever in distress, you know, from Bel's annoying teenage drama, I'll come rescue you."

It was a cute gesture, but I doubted that I'd need rescuing from Bel. I was actually looking forward to having a little sister for a bit.

"Sounds good," I laughed. "Thank you again."

"Let me throw on some sweats, and we can hang out in my room."

"Actually, your mom just heated me up some food so I think I'm going to go have a bite and then probably just turn in. I'm pretty exhausted."

Okay, that was unexpected. Not his comment, but my response. Obviously I wanted to hang out in his room. But he just seemed like he had no brake, only an accelerator. I needed some time alone to process all of this.

"I understand." He smiled and shook his head. "I still can't believe that you're here...goodnight, Maggie." He slipped past me, touching my shoulder briefly before heading back to his room.

Finally in the bathroom, I looked at myself in the mirror, shuddering at the fact that August had just seen me looking like this. The bags under my eyes were darker than normal, and my cheeks were bright red from who knows what. I was tempted to take a shower, but, as I was struggling to stay awake while washing my face, I let that thought go for now.

After I'd finally wrapped my head around the fact that I was going to be living with August, the incredibly cute bar man who I'd almost kissed and never thought I'd see again, I finished up and headed back down the hall. As I passed an open door on my right, it was slammed shut aggressively. I jumped back, startled.

Fran barely mentioned anything about the kids in the car. She most likely didn't want to overwhelm me, but she did say she had two sons, one of whom I was assuming was on the opposite side of that door slam.

The encounter quickly dampened my mood. Despite the fact that I was beyond thrilled to see August again and be able to spend more time with him, I resolved then and there to fly under the radar for a few days while I got my plans sorted out, cause no trouble whatsoever, and then get out of everybody's hair.

I joined Fran downstairs at the table, where she had placed a heaping plate of steaming lasagna on the table for me. I could get used to this type of hospitality.

As we were finishing up, the door to Fran's bedroom opened and Leone, her husband, appeared in his pajamas.

"Well, hello there." He looked slightly stunned to see me.

"Honey!" Fran jumped up from the table and hustled across the kitchen to him. "This is Maggie, the young American I told you about at the airport."

"Right, of course...Hi, Maggie." He calmly reached his hand out and I stood briefly to shake it.

"I see you've tried my lasagna," his eyes motioned toward the empty plates on the table. "It's just about the only thing I can make without burning. Fran's the true chef around here." They looked at each other and smiled.

"Yes, it was fantastic. Thank you so much, for the food, and the place to stay, and everything."

"Sure. Let us know if there's anything we can do to make you more comfortable." Both his face and voice were soft and mellow, quite the contrast from Fran's bold expressions. They do say opposites attract.

Leone kissed Fran's forehead before heading back into the bedroom. She came back to my side of the table and walked the dirty plates over to the sink.

"Can I help you with the dishes?"

She looked up and flashed me a bright, warm smile. "You need to get some rest. We're so glad you're here with us, Maggie. Sleep tight."

"You too," I responded.

When I pushed Bel's door open, she was turned away from me in her bed with headphones on watching a makeup tutorial on Youtube. I was happy she didn't seem to be in the mood to talk.

I pulled the cover up to my chin and rolled over to face the wall. I reached up and gently ran my fingers across it, picturing August laying right on the other side. I still couldn't believe it was him. I wanted to knock.

Too soon.

But, damn, he looked so hot in that towel.

I closed my eyes, reliving in exquisite detail my hallway interaction with August. His deep, Italian voice. His bare chest. His smile. Those eyes. Lips.

41

Next thing I knew, I was hearing the annoying ping of my phone alarm. I'd set it for 7am, hoping that was early enough, but I quickly realized Bel had already gone downstairs when I reached over to shut it off. I practically leapt out of bed.

Not knowing the dress code for working at a vineyard, I decided to play it safe and threw on a pair of denim shorts and a black v-neck shirt. I combed out my hair and brushed my teeth in the bathroom before putting on a pair of sandals with a thin strap around the ankle.

I was on the second to last step of the staircase when I realized I hadn't put on any makeup. Makeup was an absolute must today, as August had seen me looking pretty rough last night."

I quickly turned around and jogged back up the stairs. Having left my toiletry bag in the bathroom last night, I headed straight there. The door was slightly ajar. I grabbed the knob, and, before I could even pull, it was pushed toward me forcefully from the other side. I didn't have enough time to react, and the door collided solidly with my face.

I stumbled backwards into the wall, cupping my nose with my hands. I could feel the tears pooling in my eyes, so I tried to keep my head down to avoid looking like a complete baby.

My brothers and I used to wrestle a lot. I know they never intended to hurt me, but they never seemed to know their own strength. During one of our play fights, my older brother, Derek, got really mad at my younger brother, Sam, and tried to push me out of the way so they could go at it. He pushed me so hard that I flew into the coffee table and broke my nose. I thought it was never going to stop bleeding.

This was right around the time of my parents' divorce. I remember they were literally fighting about who should take me to the hospital. Derek ended up driving me. Sam came too. They both sat with me practically all night while I cried a lot and held ice on my face to stop the swelling. It really freaked them out that they had hurt me. They won't even arm wrestle with me now.

I saw different ENT specialists for years to try and fix my nose-bleeding problem caused by my collision with the table. But still, to this day, if my nose is hit hard enough and in the right spot, it will bleed for hours.

The tears poured down my face, not because it really hurt that much, but because the smell and the taste of blood brought me right back to that day when I cried and bled until there were no more tears or blood left.

"Jesus, watch where you're going!" He looked at me and saw the blood pouring down my face. "Shit...are you OK?" His tone sharply shifted.

"Um...yeah. I think so. I...just hope my nose isn't broken again." I was trying to position my hands to keep the blood from hitting the floor. I looked up at him for a brief second. He was really good-looking. He looked like a combination of August and Bel.

"Again?"

"Yeah...it's kind of a thing with me. I just need to get it to stop bleeding. I'll be fine. I'm just going to go get cleaned up." I carefully maneuvered around him and closed the door to the bathroom behind me before I could embarrass myself any further.

I started running the water to get it warm and pinched the bridge of my nose. This was a trick that one of my many doctors had told me would "work like a charm every time." Well, Doc, my 10 years of chronic nose bleeds beg to differ.

I stuffed a tissue up my nose so that I could rinse off my hands and face without more blood rushing out. Despite having dealt with this issue since childhood, I still got really freaked out when I saw my blood pooling in the sink.

I started to feel dizzy, and then I was falling backwards. I managed to brace my hands on the bathtub behind me as I fell, and then the bathroom lights quickly went dark.

When I woke up, my eyes felt incredibly heavy. I rubbed them vigorously in an attempt to figure out where the hell I was. A figure slowly started to come into focus. I attempted to sit up in the bed, which was, apparently, slightly ambitious as I couldn't even make it halfway up without collapsing back down again.

"Whoa there, let's just stay down for a little longer. You're okay, just relax."

His calm tone washed all my concerns away. In one hand, he held a bag of frozen corn; with his other hand, he held mine. I was pretty content to stay like this forever. But...something wasn't right...

"August...why am I in your bed?" I kept my eyes closed and spoke as loudly as I could without adding to the throbbing in my head.

"Ms. Maggie, please get your mind out of the gutter. My room is closer to the bathroom than yours. The same bathroom where you just fainted and left a trail of blood on the floor."

"I fainted!?" My eyes opened widely.

"Yes. We were getting breakfast set up downstairs and heard a loud thud. Nic looked very guilty when he entered the kitchen, and I knew you were still upstairs, so I told everyone I'd come up to make sure you were alright. I knocked on the bathroom door and there was no answer so I went in, and there you were, lying on the bathroom floor, blood everywhere. I picked you up, and I brought you in here. You've been out for about 5 minutes or so. Are you okay?"

Knowing the entire family had heard my "loud thud," as August so generously called it, was horrifying. I squeezed my eyes shut, wanting to basically disappear.

"Your brother and I had a little...accident involving the bathroom door."

"Yeah, I figured it was something like that. That's the other Costelli brother, Nic. Much angrier, way less attractive."

I appreciated his attempt to make me laugh, but I couldn't help replaying the encounter with Nic. That wasn't exactly how I wanted to meet the final family member.

"August, I'm okay. I just need a minute. I'll be down right away." I could feel his hesitation to leave; his eyes remained laser-focused on me.

"Are you sure you're okay? I can stay."

"Seriously. I'll be there in a few. I'm fine. Go." I squeezed his hand this time. This seemed to show him I meant it. He stood up and began to head toward the door.

"Maggie?" He called back to me.

"Yeah?" I propped myself up onto my elbows.

"Don't scare me like that again."

I smiled and fell back onto the pillow. I could feel him still standing there watching me before I finally heard the door close gently.

I gradually made my way to the bathroom to clean up the disgusting mess I must've made. Steadying myself using the wall, I rounded the corner to the bathroom to find it spotless. Sparkling clean.

I don't remember falling, but I do remember my blood, lots of it, all over the sink and the floor.

It had to have been August. The thought of him cleaning up my blood was equally gross and charming. I looked in the mirror and couldn't control the huge smile that overtook my face.

This guy was unreal.

I washed my hands and applied some concealer to the bruise already forming around my upper nose/eye region. Hopefully this wouldn't be a big topic of discussion downstairs. The thought that I was causing this much of a ruckus on my first official day here was more painful than my headache.

I set my phone on my bed in Bel's room and walked downstairs where I was instantly halted by the scene I witnessed at the kitchen table.

When I was younger, even before the split, my family and I rarely ate meals together. Sometimes, if our schedules aligned, we would catch each other for dinner, but I mostly ate in my room. It was the only place I could get peace and quiet. Which was the exact opposite of what I had just walked into.

August and Bel were shouting at each other playfully, switching between Italian and English while they passed large plates of pancakes and bacon back and forth. Did they do this every morning, or were they just trying to impress me?

Leone looked a lot different now that I was able to see him in actual clothes. He was extremely tall and thin, which explained where all the kids got their height. His hair was long but well styled, that purposefully messy look you can never get without a professional. He read the morning paper as he sipped his coffee. *Typical dad.*

Once they noticed me standing there, all conversation and activity stopped and everyone stared at me.

Fran immediately jumped up and ran over to me. "Sweetie…are you ok?! She ran her thumbs across my forehead and observed my tiny wound.

"Yes, I'm fine. Just clumsy." There was no point in going into detail about what had happened with Nic. After all, it was an accident. I think.

"Do you want some ibuprofen? Maybe you should just take it easy today. You can start working tomorrow."

"Gosh, no. I'm seriously fine, Fran! I will take some ibuprofen, though. And I'm sure a pancake or two wouldn't hurt." I winked at her.

She motioned for me to take a seat at the table before quickly shuffling to a cabinet next to the fridge and pulling out a large basket of assorted pill containers. I sat down and took a deep breath.

Bel passed me the platter of bacon. "Here. Bacon cures everything."

Leone looked up ever so slightly from his newspaper and offered me a warm smile. He definitely seemed like a man of few words.

Fran returned with a glass of water in one hand and two pills in the other. She set them down and then went to pour me a cup of coffee.

Nic wasn't in the kitchen. Was he already outside working?

August nudged me. "Are you feeling okay?" He spoke softly.

"Yes, I'm fine. Did you clean up the bathroom, or did I do that?"

"There was barely anything to clean. Don't worry." He took a long sip from his mug, shifting his gaze away from me. I appreciated how little attention he was drawing to the subject.

"Thanks."

He nodded without looking at me.

After we all had finished eating, Fran commanded our attention.

"Alright, up up up kids. Let's get moving! Maggie's the only one with an excuse to take it easy out there today. This vineyard isn't going to run itself."

She started to tickle Bel until she stood and started heading for the side door. August protested as he grabbed another pancake for the road.

I laughed at them trying to resist Fran because she was obviously going to get her way. I followed behind them, determined to make myself useful after my humiliating morning.

CHAPTER FOUR

"Guys, get started over there. You know what to do. I'm going to show Maggie around."

The bright sun shone down on the vineyard, which seemed to go on for miles. I paused for a moment to marvel at its vastness now that I could actually see it in the daylight. There were rows and rows of vines stretching across acres of rolling fields. Four large, barn-like structures sat on the edge of a thick forest behind the house. Each one was a different pastel color and had a slightly different shape. This place was so magical; I felt like I was in a painting.

Fran led me over to a wooden shed which had dozens of multi-colored hand prints of all sizes plastered across the side. Most of them had names and dates scribbled next to them.

"Alright, Maggie, this is sort of headquarters for the vineyard. We call it home base," Fran said as we circled the shed. "The handprints are from family, friends, visitors...it's sort of like an interactive guest book, so we can remember everyone who got to come and enjoy our beautiful vineyard that we've worked so long to build." She opened both doors wide.

"Here is where we keep all the supplies. If you ever need anything, it's probably in here somewhere." There were different sections of tools and equipment, all perfectly organized and labeled.

"Now, once a week we all take turns organizing home base. It can get pretty messy with all of us going in and out grabbing stuff. This, over here, is our main schedule to show who's cleaning what and when."

She pointed to the back of the shed door where there was a color-coded schedule packed full of tasks for each family member.

"Usually, it's just Leone and me and Nic out here. Bel only works on weekends because of school. When August got home from London, I added him onto the schedule, but now he'll be having virtual school, as will Bel, so he'll mostly just be working on weekends too. Both of their schools are closed now for a week so we have some extra help for a little while. What's going on with your university?"

I had completely forgotten about school before she said this. "That's a great question. We haven't heard the plan from the university yet. I'll let you know what ends up happening but I can work as much as you need until then."

She nodded while throwing her hair back into a ponytail. I looked up at the schedule and squinted as I tried to get a grasp of what the hell I'd be doing. I think Fran could tell I was slightly overwhelmed by the sight of it when she put her arm around my shoulder.

"Don't worry. You'll get the hang of it. Your color is yellow. But I took it easy on you and only gave you a few tasks for this first week. Since it's so early in the season, there's not a ton to do; right now the biggest task is to prune the vines. Hopefully you don't mind getting a little dirty." She squeezed my shoulder pulling me into a tight side hug.

"I want to help as much as possible. Seriously, if you need to put me on there more, I can handle it." She shook her head as she straightened a shovel hanging on the wall.

"We're going to start you off with this for now. I don't want any more accidents. Plus, I rarely have all three kids home at the same time so this is a lot more help than we're used to!"

I snuck a quick glance at the schedule, trying to see if I'd been assigned any tasks with a certain someone. Before I could get a good look, Fran was calling me from outside the shed, and I hustled out to her, shutting the doors gingerly behind me.

"Fran, when did you and Leone open the vineyard?"

"Oh boy, that's a long story. Here, why don't we sit down for a minute. It'll be good for you to know the history of the vineyard in case any customers have questions. They tend to find us on google and just show up, hoping we'll drop everything and take them on a tour. Brides are a pain. I wouldn't be surprised if we get a bride or two even during this quarantine."

I sat down next to her on a bench outside the shed.

"The vineyard has been in our family for almost 60 years now. My parents bought it a few years after they got married; it was nothing but 20 acres of empty land at that point. They worked their entire lives on it." She was gazing at the property wistfully.

"I grew up working here and helping them in any way I could. I actually met Leone here too. He was hired as extra summer staff to help set up tents and stuff for parties and weddings. We had a lot of fun that summer." She leaned into me and gave me a sly smile.

"Leone had always dreamed of moving to the US. He grew up with very little and wanted a fresh start far, far away. He also didn't have much family. His mother died when he was young, and he's an only child. So he was really eager to start a family of his own, which was just one of the many reasons I fell for him so quickly. After about a year of dating, Leone asked me to come with him to the US...scared the hell out of me. This tiny countryside town in rural Italy was all I'd ever known. I never even had a job that wasn't working here for my parents."

"What did your parents say?" I interjected.

"Of course they thought it was absurd. Which it was. Leone was so easygoing and adventurous and always pushing me to do things that were out of my comfort zone, and I absolutely loved him for it. He really changed my life." The way she lit up when she talked about Leone gave me butterflies. It was as if the love she had for him radiated off her so that anyone nearby could feel it too.

"So, long story short, we moved to the US and into the tiniest one bedroom apartment you've ever seen in Maplewood, New Jersey, of all places. I was 21 and he was 24 at the time. He had a cousin that lived in New York City, and this was the closest we could get to him without spending every penny we'd saved up on rent alone. We stayed in New Jersey for about 10 years. That's where both Nic and August were born. I was really happy they got to experience American childhoods; that's something that Bel always gives us a hard time about. She wants to visit the US so badly, but we just haven't found the right time for her yet. We've been thinking maybe an exchange program or even possibly college over there for her. We think she would fit in perfectly."

"She definitely would," I added. "So why did you end up moving back here?"

"Well, my dad had Alzheimers that progressed quickly, and my mom started talking about selling the vineyard because she was afraid she wouldn't be able to take care of it on her own. She even put it on the market and had a few potential buyers. Believe it or not, at that point, I really didn't care too much. I had made peace with losing the vineyard, and I just wanted my mom to be happy. But Leone was terribly upset by this. He went on and on about how this was where we first met and fell in love, and we couldn't just hand it off to some stranger who would do god-knows-what with it. And he was right. It was home. So he insisted we rush back immediately and stop my mom from selling it to anyone."

"Wow. Was it hard to persuade her not to sell it?"

"You know, I was getting tired of the smell of New Jersey, and the kids were old enough at that point to make the move back not so difficult on us, so we persuaded my mom to take it off the market and told her we would take care of everything for her and dad. She was ecstatic. Shortly after we moved back we had Bel, and the rest is history."

"That's amazing. I had no idea this place had such a romantic story behind it. You've made it so beautiful." I looked out and saw all three kids working in the distance. I felt a sudden pang of jealousy after hearing Fran's story.

"Ever since we took it over, we've just tried each year to improve things and add on to make it more successful. Like, for instance, we didn't have any barns back then. We built them over the years as we noticed the demand for wedding and event spaces was increasing. And my parents never even considered selling the wine anywhere but here; we've really tried to branch out and market ourselves to the most people possible. That's why I was so upset when our investor put us on hold. We've worked so hard, and this damn virus just feels like a step backwards. But overall, it still feels like the place I grew up and met the love of my life and raised my beautiful children. I just thank God that Leone didn't let me let my mom sell it." I noticed a tear in her eye as she spoke.

"Because then, you never would've met me," I winked at her, trying to lighten the mood.

"Exactly. I'm very glad you're here, Maggie." She rubbed my back.

"Me too."

"Well, enough of the sappy stuff. Let's get moving; there's work to be done!" She held out her hand to help me up and we began walking over to meet the others working on the vines.

As we walked together in silence, I was reveling in everything that Fran had shared. The fact that Leone wouldn't let her sell this place because it's where they met and fell in love had to be one of the dreamiest things I'd ever heard. I had never even seen my parents hold hands or kiss on the lips, so this declaration of love was completely foreign to me.

Fran gave me a quick step-by-step tutorial on pruning and dropped me off in one of the rows next to Nic. I got started immediately. I was hoping he and I could start over after our not-so-graceful encounter this morning.

Before Fran left us, she walked over to Nic, motioning for him to remove his headphones. She leaned in to him, saying something that I couldn't hear. After she stopped talking, Nic gave her a sullen nod and put his headphones back on.

What's his deal?

"Have fun you two, and take lots of water breaks!"

Nic didn't look up. He probably didn't even hear what she'd said; I could hear the music from his headphones even this far away.

We worked silently for the first hour or so. I couldn't stop daydreaming about the story Fran had just told me. What a Fran and Leone kind of love must feel like and how it overcame your every move and you couldn't do anything without considering how it would affect the person you love. Reliving her story in my head made working with Nic more tolerable.

I snuck a few glances at him, observing the way he worked. He was like a machine, with no wasted effort or movement. He seemed to know instantly the best place to cut the vines; he clipped them so fast, I didn't know how he could even tell what he was doing, and he didn't look up once. His black messy hair flopped around and sweat dripped down his face before he combatively wiped it away. He was in better shape than August, if that was possible, I guess because of all the work he did here at the vineyard.

I was determined to focus on the vines and stay quiet, hoping to not have any more negative interactions with him.

To be honest, I was a little surprised he still hadn't apologized for knocking me practically unconscious this morning. Maybe he thinks it was my fault?

I typically enjoyed silence, but silence around Nic was different. It was somehow incredibly loud and shoved in your face. Like he couldn't even be the least bit pleasant?

I survived Nic's moodiness all day and decided that headphones were a must tomorrow.

When we were just about done for the day, I decided to go back to home base to look at the schedule. I was desperate to know who I'd be working with the rest of the week, praying that it was anyone other than Nic.

As I started to make my way there, I tripped over a pile of tangled vines and literally face planted straight down into the dirt. I lay there for a second, shocked and embarrassed, before using my shirt to attempt to wipe the dirt out of my eyes.

Refusing to turn around and check if Nic had just seen my accident, I suddenly heard a deep belly laugh erupt from behind me. I whipped my body around and saw Nic reaching into his pocket.

Before I could even stand, he quickly snapped a picture of me with a disposable camera.

Who the hell even uses those things anymore?

It's like he had it with him specifically anticipating that I was going to do something stupid and worthy of documenting. I really wanted to lunge after him and grab the camera, but he was already running back to the house. Laughing uncontrollably. At least it's good to know he's capable of smiling, even if it's at my expense.

I stood up and brushed myself off. The thought of him showing that picture to his friends while they all sat around and made fun of the clumsy American tourist was enough to make me want to hide in my room and never come back out.

I walked back toward the house with my head hung low, covered in both dirt and embarrassment. I just hoped nobody would be in the kitchen to see me like this. I couldn't stop glancing down at my filthy clothes.

Perfect.

Day one and I've already bled all over the place, fainted, tripped and overall made a damn fool of myself.

CHAPTER FIVE

I made my way into the kitchen, practically tiptoeing, hoping not to get anything dirty. I picked up speed on the stairs and rushed to the bathroom. I found Bel standing at the mirror doing her makeup. Seemed kind of pointless to me while stuck in quarantine, but she looked absolutely gorgeous.

Bel glanced at me as I entered. "What the hell happened to you out there?"

I stepped further into the bathroom and shut the door quickly.

"My first day here and I'm already making messes all over the place." I didn't even know where to start to clean myself up, so I sunk down onto the floor and covered my head with my hands.

Bel laughed, clearly not one for attending pity parties. She sank down next to me in solidarity.

"Come on, miss drama queen…I bet nobody even saw."

"Do you think I'd be this embarrassed if nobody was there? Bel, your brother was standing 10 feet away. He took a picture of me!"

"Oh my god. I'm totally making him print me a copy of that picture."

I rolled my eyes, and gave her shoulder a push.

"What's his deal anyway?"

"God, I'm so glad someone else sees it too! He's so stuck up now that he studies film in London and thinks he's the next Tarantino."

I couldn't help but laugh. "Tarantino, huh? I pegged him for more of a musical guy...like Lin-Manuel, 'cause let's be honest, he's not badass enough to be Tarantino."

She burst into laughter. I was pleasantly surprised that she got my subtle Hamilton reference, especially since she had never even been to America.

"But no, I meant Nic. August actually has been really sweet and welcoming to me, but Nic...jeez, I feel like he just doesn't want me here."

She shifted her body to face me.

"Yeah, he's a tough one. I don't know how to talk to him...nobody does...well, except his two bonehead friends Jack and Elliott, who rotate sharing the same single brain cell. He seems to have a soft spot for them," she added. "He isn't a bad guy, but he's been through some shit."

"What do you mean?"

Bel hesitated. "Look, it's not my place to talk about it and it has nothing to do with you, so I wouldn't worry about it. The guy just has some issues, that's all."

I had a terrible habit of trying to figure people out and then fix them. My friends always called the boys I dated my "projects." But I'm not sure I could fix someone with an attitude like Nic's.

"He barely talks to me; normally he's just telling me to get out of his room and shut the door behind me. I've gotten used to it though, and you will too...My best piece of advice is to just stay out of his way. That's what we've all started to do, anyway."

Bel pulled over the trash can and giggled to herself as she brushed away the residue of my latest embarrassment.

"Let's stop talking about that loser. I want to hear more about our esteemed guest. What's America like, anyway? My stupid parents won't let me go until I'm older."

Gee, how does one describe America.

"Yeah, Fran told me you've never been. Let's see...America is, um, nice I guess. It's crowded, in some places more than others, and it's loud, but not so much where I live. I grew up in Michigan, a state almost completely surrounded by big lakes called the 5 great lakes. It's sort of what makes us famous. People travel from all over to spend summertime there and it's a tradition to go "up north" in Michigan during the summer."

"Wow, so your state attracts many tourists, sort of like our country." She winked at me, almost condescendingly, but I could tell it was in good faith. I hoped she wouldn't think of me as a tourist for long.

"You'd love Northern Michigan in the summer. It's kind of similar to here actually, lots of vineyards and cherry orchards. It's always been my dream to work on a vineyard; that's why I practically leaped into your mom's car when she offered to let me come stay here."

"Yeah, speaking of that. Do you make a habit of going to stranger's homes directly after meeting them for the first time?"

I burst out laughing. I seriously couldn't get over how much I enjoyed this girl's lack of filter when she talked.

"I usually have more nerves and apprehension when it comes to making big decisions like this one, but there was just something so warm and welcoming about your mom. She made me feel safe, like I could definitely trust her, even though I didn't know her at all."

"Yeah, sounds like Fran. She's always been like that. My friends love coming over here because she always feeds us and lets us have some wine if we beg hard enough. When Dad said she was bringing back an American tourist, I didn't even flinch."

"That's exactly what August said last night!"

"Mom clearly has a bit of a reputation. You'll learn to love her and her craziness. I guarantee it."

"I love how close you all are as a family. It kind of makes me jealous. Mine is the opposite, which was a big reason I didn't feel a huge inclination to go back home when my friends left. My family is a shit show...pardon my language."

"There have been times I've thought about running away to a foreign country too. Everything isn't always as perfect and shiny as it looks on the outside, you know."

Bel looked way older than 16. She had beautiful, long, dirty blonde hair that was naturally pin-straight, of course. She was tall too. All of them were except for Fran. I still felt like a midget walking amongst them.

Bel stood up and reached her hand out for me to grab.

"Speaking of my close family, don't go getting any ideas about getting too close. I promise, both Costelli boys are a BIG waste of your time."

I took her hand and stood up. I was thrown off by her warning not to get involved with her brothers. She put her hand on my cheek jokingly.

"You're too pretty for them anyway, dirt and all." She lowered her hand from my face and blew an air kiss as she exited the bathroom.

"Thank you for talking me down," I called to her as she was leaving. "I'll pay you back somehow, I promise."

Bel poked her head back in the bathroom and whispered to me. "Pay me back by staying away from those losers I have to call brothers." She started down the hall. "See you downstairs for dinner," she called back to me as she ran down the stairs.

Why was Bel so adamant that I shouldn't get involved with Nic or August? I mean, obviously I wasn't going to get involved with Nic. But why not August? He seemed almost perfect. Was her warning too late?

I shook my head as I viewed my dusty image in the mirror. I washed my face and headed back to my room to change clothes and lay down before dinner, vowing, once again, to stay out of Nic's way. Why did it seem like every time I got near him, something crazy happened? And not in a good way.

After I changed my clothes, I decided to call Bec and Jen. I didn't have the energy to go into much detail with them, but I knew they were probably desperate for an update by now. Plus, navigating the time difference would be difficult so I had to take advantage of the small windows of free time I could find. I started a group FaceTime call, and both of them answered during the first ring.

"Maggie! Are you okay? What happened to your face? Where are you?" Bec pressed before I had a chance to even say hello. Jen just smiled and looked genuinely pleased to see me still alive.

"Hi guys. Yes, I'm okay. It's kind of a long story, and I don't have much time right now to explain, but I'm staying on a vineyard with a woman I met at the airport. She's letting me work here for a bit until the virus calms down."

"You're...at a vineyard? With a random woman you met at the airport? Do you know how crazy you sound right now? Please make this make sense for us."

I couldn't help but laugh. It did sound clinically insane when I said it out loud.

"I know it sounds strange, but I promise Fran is trustworthy. She just wanted me to be safe so she invited me to come stay here. She has three kids...one of whom...you may know."

"What do you mean one we may know?" Jen interjected.

"Well..."

"You're joking." Bec's face shifted from concerned to even more concerned, her forehead creasing deeply.

I remained quiet.

Of course she knew who I was talking about. Who else would we all know from around here? I just didn't want to say it out loud; honestly I was still trying to grapple with the fact myself.

"Are you lying to us about this Fran lady? Did you get his number at the club the other night? Did he ask you to stay with him? Did he do that to your face?"

I immediately turned down my phone volume in case there was

anyone nearby listening to her intrusive questioning.

"Jesus, Bec, calm down. That's ridiculous. I would never just stay with some random guy I met at a club. It's just the most unbelievable coincidence in the world. And no, he didn't do this to my face. I ran into...a door." I couldn't help but let out a small chuckle at the thought of my own clumsiness.

She wasn't even trying to hide the fact that she didn't believe me when she hit me with the biggest eye roll in the world.

"Wait, so the pushy bar guy is Fran's son?" Jen broke up the tension. She didn't sound as concerned, just astonished.

"Yes! Isn't that insane? His name is August. He was in the city last night because he's back home from college. Fran wanted all the kids to be home safe in case the virus got really bad and they couldn't leave for a while. When I saw him coming out of the bathroom last night, I think my breathing stopped completely."

"What are the odds..." Bec sarcastically muttered under her breath.

"Guys, I promise to keep you updated and fill you in on the details, but I have to go right now. I am okay, I am safe, and I will talk to you very soon." I tried to aim this reassurance at Bec, but she still seemed skeptical.

"We love you, Mag. So glad you're safe." Jen smiled warmly.

"Thanks. I love you both. Talk soon."

"Love you, Maggie," Bec added, which made me feel slightly better.

I set my phone down and closed my eyes. Bec drove me nuts, but all her concern was rooted in love. I smiled to myself, thinking about my besties.

But almost immediately, Bel's words came back into my head. Smile gone.

To me, August was this sexy, funny, sweet, smart, incredibly hot man who was giving me pretty clear signals that he was interested. To her, he was her idiot brother.

I didn't actually tell her that I wouldn't get involved with him, though. She just told me not to. And she is a sixteen year-old child -- granted, one who seems wiser than most adults I know -- but, still. Ugh! I really didn't want to go behind Bel's back, but I wanted him so bad.

I took a long deep breath.

As I made my way downstairs for dinner, I decided to give myself a little mental pep talk: I...Magnolia Akers...will figure this out. I can resist him...I can...and I will...I think...*shit*.

CHAPTER SIX

One Week Later

Each day, I told myself I was going to try and find a place to stay in the city, but the days working outside were so long; I barely had enough energy to chat with Bel at the end of the day before completely passing out from exhaustion.

Fran kept insisting that I stay at the vineyard as long as possible, so I just worked really hard to show my gratitude for their hospitality. I had no idea one could get so sore from pruning grape vines.

The virus had also been getting increasingly worse. Pretty much the entire country was now shut down, and, from the little bit of news I'd watched, it seemed like everyone was starting to freak out about it. It wasn't too bad in the US yet but, given our current "leadership," it was only a matter of time.

My dad finally called me back a few days after I left him the voicemail of all voicemails. He took it better than I thought he would. He left me a message while I was outside working.

Hey Mag! How are you doing? Thanks for letting me know you're not coming back quite yet. I feel like as a parent I should be more concerned about this, but I trust you completely. You've always been the responsible one, and you deserve to live a little. But please stay safe. Love you, always.

My mom, surprisingly, didn't call and scream at me either. She texted me a lengthy paragraph a few hours after the message from my dad came in. Ten percent of the text consisted of her attempts at being a concerned parent, while the other ninety percent was her telling me about the vacation she and Roger were planning now that they were working remotely due to the virus.

I skimmed through it quickly and didn't reply. Having emotionally distant parents can pay off in situations like this. You don't have to deal with begging for their permission to do the things you want to do. I'm sure my future therapist will have a field day with comments like that.

I could tell the weekends here would be generally relaxing and peaceful, for me at least. Fran told me that I would be expected to help with a few chores on Saturday morning and would have the rest of the weekend to myself.

Tonight, I was about to experience one of the famous Costelli parties that Bel had told me about. She said Fran is known for hosting every holiday and special occasion here at the house. We were in quarantine, of course, but that didn't seem to be stopping her from finding a reason to celebrate. I aspire to someday achieve her level of optimism.

She had vowed to plan a differently themed dinner for each Friday night. Tonight's theme was "prom." Obviously, I didn't pack anything remotely close to a prom dress, so I chose a black off-the-shoulder sundress, jazzed it up with some sparkly jewelry, and hoped that would do.

When I came downstairs, I was blown away by Fran's decorating skills. She had black and gold balloons hanging from each corner of the living room and white streamers hanging from the ceiling. I was slightly confused about where she'd gotten all the supplies when all the stores in town were closed until I remembered that she does own a wedding venue and must have tons of extra decorations laying around.

Fran handed me a crystal flute of champagne as soon as I entered the kitchen.

"Welcome to the 2020 Covid-19 Costelli Prom. You look absolutely lovely, my dear."

"Fran, this is amazing! You are so talented. And you look gorgeous."

Fran was wearing a purple and green satin shift dress with three-quarter sleeves, gold chandelier earrings, and purple Birkenstock sandals.

Bel was lying on the couch looking at her phone. She was wearing a pink bustier with a purple taffeta calf-length skirt and Doc Martens boots. Her hair was in a top-knot around which was tied a black ribbon.

August instantaneously made his way over to me. He glided

across the floor effortlessly in a black, perfectly fitted suit with a burgundy tie. He pushed his hair back behind his ear with one hand, while his other hand remained snug in his pocket.

The way he walked over with such confidence reminded me of the first night we met at Silk.

"Maggie." He bowed his head slightly with a smirk.

"August."

"You look…" He studied me slowly, starting at my collarbone, moving down to my ankles, and finally meeting my eyes. "Fucking amazing."

I honestly felt like I was standing in front of him completely naked. That's how he made me feel when he looked at me like that.

"As do you."

This was an understatement. He looked ridiculously hot; the suit was killing me. It hugged his body in all the right places, and the burgundy color made his eyes literally sparkle.

August and I hadn't really had much alone time over the past week, which, frankly, was only adding to the tension building between us. He was always looking at me though: across the breakfast table, while we were working, watching TV at night. I had to fight every urge in my body not to look back at him because every time I did, like right now, I could feel my face flush.

He took a long sip of his beer.

"Did you go to your high school prom?"

"Prom was…a joke." I tried to quickly dismiss the topic.

"Oh yeah?" He sounded intrigued. "Let's hear about it."

"My boyfriend at the time was a narcissistic jerk. When he

realized I wasn't going to sleep with him that night, he broke up with me on the spot. And he didn't just break up with me. He threw a grown-ass temper tantrum." We both started laughing. "He called me the "prom prude" until we graduated."

"I'm sorry that happened. Girls like you deserve to feel special at their one and only prom."

Girls like me.

I tried to decipher what exactly that meant as I shrugged my shoulders. It was such a distant memory that I felt no grief over it.

"Did you enjoy yours?"

He hesitated and took another long sip of his beer. "Well, here in Italy we don't call it "prom" exactly. It's a dance still, but, instead, it's referred to as "I cento giorni" or "the one hundred days." It takes place one hundred days before our final exams."

I nodded, eager to learn more about their life and culture here.

"Anyways, I wouldn't use the word, "enjoy." You see, I took a family friend, Lucy. I had always had a crush on her growing up, and I thought that night might be my chance to finally make a move. Well, we had a great time for about an hour, and then she said she wanted to dance with her friends. So I said fine, I'll go get a drink for us. So I'm waiting in line to get us something to drink, and this guy goes, 'Hey, August, look over there.' I looked over, and there she was. Not just dancing with, but kissing, my goddamn brother. Nic had somehow made his move and gotten her all to himself. I just left. I was furious with him. Of course, he had some story about her throwing herself at him. Bullshit. And she said she was so drunk that she didn't even remember being with him. I haven't spoken to either of them about it since. They can both go to hell as far as I'm concerned."

I tried to picture someone, anyone, turning August down like that. Especially for Nic. August was warm and kind and sweet and predictable, while Nic seemed anything but. That Lucy girl had made a big mistake.

Speaking of Nic, he was apparently not engaging with the theme of the evening. He stood leaning against the fridge on his phone. He had on basketball shorts and a black sweatshirt. He looked annoyed and brooding, per usual.

I snapped back to the handsome man standing in front of me.

I held my glass up to initiate a quiet toast. "Time to put the past in the past. Here's to making new and improved prom memories tonight."

He smiled broadly as he clinked his glass against mine.

"August, Maggie, Bel, Nic, come here! We're going to take a picture before we sit down for dinner." Fran had constructed a make-shift photo booth out of poster board and had her camera on a tripod. The lengths to which this woman would go to ensure we had fun was heartwarming.

We hurried over to join her. Leone, who had appeared out of nowhere in a black suit with a white shirt and black bow tie, was already posed in front of the backdrop that read, "Costelli COVID-19 Prom 2020." I think my favorite thing about this family was that they knew how to make even the worst circumstances seem not so bad. Most families, like mine, would sulk and complain about being stuck inside together for a few weeks. But not the Costelli's.

Nic finally looked up from his phone and saw all of us trying to fit into the camera frame. He was out the side door so fast that Fran didn't even have time to yell at him to stay. Nobody ever seemed phased when Nic disappeared over and over again.

Where the hell did he go?

"Alright everyone...say prom night!" Fran set the timer and jogged over to join the group, squeezing in just before the shutter clicked. I felt a familiar hand slide around my waist and pull me closer into the frame. I don't think I've ever smiled harder in a photo before.

Fran immediately transferred the photos from her camera to her laptop so she could post them on Facebook. She asked if she could tag me in them. I think she was hoping my family would see and trust that I was in good hands.

The photos were cute so I didn't mind. Plus, I knew Bec and Jen would have a field day once they saw them.

We sat down for dinner. Fran brought out plate after plate of delicious-looking food. First, pasta e fagioli, a soupy concoction of noodles, beans, and vegetables. Then, meatballs in a red sauce. And finally, a chilled caprese salad. I'm sure you've seen movies where big, loud, Italian families feast on course after course and drown it all with copious amounts of red wine. Well...that's pretty much what a Friday night at the Costelli's looked like, except this particular Friday, everyone looked so fancy and beautiful.

Especially August.

Growing up, my parents had always been incredibly conservative. They definitely believed in never supplying alcohol to their underage daughter. Not even a tiny glass of wine.

The Costelli's, in contrast, clearly didn't care if I had a glass, or two, or three, and that freedom was just as intoxicating as the wine. Fran raised the bottle countless times to see if anyone needed a refill, and my glass always seemed to be the first one up.

The dessert, a handmade cannoli with velvety vanilla filling and chocolate shavings, was heavenly. As I was savoring it and listening to Bel and August argue over whose turn it was to clean up, my thoughts wandered to my own siblings.

Sam and Derek were really protective of me when I was little. I loved it. I felt invincible with them around. Besides wrestling and getting nosebleeds, I basically just tagged along with whatever they were doing...when they would let me.

We played football in the backyard, they taught me how to shoot my first paintball gun, and we went snake hunting. Once, we snuck into this old, abandoned house that everyone said was haunted -- I was only seven -- my brothers got in so much trouble for taking me in there. I loved being one of the guys, but there was such a big age gap between us...Derek went to college when I was in 4th grade. And Sam went three years later. So I just didn't see them much after that.

Derek owns a landscaping company and still lives fairly near us. He is married to Carissa, who is the sweetest person you could ever meet. She's a pediatric nurse and pretty much the human form of sunshine. They have a German Shepherd named Jackson and I'm pretty sure they'll be trying for a baby, or five, here soon. That reminds me; I should call them. I'm sure she's having a difficult time working in the healthcare field during a freaking pandemic.

Sam moved to Grand Rapids a few years ago. He's a high school math teacher. He's very single, and I don't think that will be changing for a while. Sam is a tough one to nail down. He's never been much of a people person.

You wouldn't be able to tell we're siblings from looking at us. They're both incredibly athletic and muscular, while I'm quite literally the opposite. I'm just shy of 5'3" and have the strength of a semi-active geriatric who does water aerobics once a month.

After my brothers moved out, my family grew apart. To say the least. I still talk to my brothers fairly regularly but nothing like when we were kids. Time, distance, divorce...oh my.

I had accepted I would never have a tight-knit family, and, frankly, I never desired one until I saw the Costelli's. I sort of thought everyone's family felt fractured.

I felt jealous almost, sitting here watching this family -- well most of them -- (Where the hell was Nic? And why did no one seem to care?) obviously enjoying each others' company. I promised myself I wouldn't take for granted a single moment I was here. I was going to soak up every ounce of quality family time I could get because I knew I would long for this when I returned back to my regular life.

I didn't realize how long I'd been in my own little world until August yelled at me from across the table at an obnoxious volume.

"Maggie! Dance with me! Come on!"

He was slurring his words a bit, but not too bad. His tie was loosened around his neck now, and his collar was relaxed. He swayed with the music.

August's style was incredibly simple; he never wore anything other than basic, dark colors, and no designs or patterns. It worked wonders for him. Tonight, he looked like James Bond. But like Italian and way sexier.

I tried to let him down easy.

"I have two left feet. Dancing is not something you want to see me do."

His nose scrunched with dissatisfaction. "I'll be the judge of that."

"Yes, dancing! Everyone up! I'll show you all to the dance floor!" Fran signaled us to follow her into the living room. Of course, she'd thought of creating a dance floor. Fran must've had a hand in planning her 100 days dance back in the day. She was too good at this.

Fran hit play on the TV remote and "Smooth Criminal" by Michael Jackson boomed through the speakers. Leone grabbed Bel and twirled her around and then dipped her. She let out a scream as she arched back.

August reached his hand out and pulled me in. I made sure to keep a few inches between us. I had no idea what I was doing and neither did my feet, but August was so smooth that he almost made up for it. We floated around the living room for a few songs, both of us cracking up when I, of course, tripped on his feet.

Thankfully, Fran cut in. I walked back into the kitchen to get a drink of water, letting them have a family moment.

I grabbed a glass from the cupboard, filled it with water from the fridge, and leaned against the counter. I took a long sip.

As I set the empty glass down, a hand slid across my lower back and around to my waist. That familiar hand. That body heat. I turned to face him.

"Two left feet, huh? Looked pretty good to me."

I smiled stiffly, uncomfortable with the amount of affection he was displaying with his family so close.

"Come with me," he whispered.

Did he really just say that?

Was he really flirting with me so blatantly with his family in the next room? The dancing could easily be passed off as a friendly gesture, but this. This was definitely not just friendly.

I gently pushed him away to a more appropriate distance, which I could tell caught him off guard.

"I can't. Not now at least." I whispered back to him. Your family is right in there; they would notice if we left."

He leaned in closer. "I told mom that I was going to show you the back patio. Just trust me."

I highly doubted that he had actually had that conversation with Fran. I looked at him with a raised eyebrow.

"I promise, Maggie. Come on!"

Oh, what the hell. What's the worst thing that can happen on a patio?

"Fine, but patio better not be code word for something else. Just think of my friend Bec and how disappointed she'd be in you."

He laughed. "Oh my. How could I forget the tiny-but-mighty Bec. I will try never to disappoint her."

He took my hand and led me out the side door and around to

the back patio. I couldn't believe that I hadn't been out here at night yet. There were white lights hung between four tall poles, one on each corner, creating almost a ceiling above the stone patio. Gorgeous, hand-painted lanterns lined the edge of a path that led around the house.

The crisp air made me shiver.

"Here." August took off his jacket and placed it around my shoulders.

Cliche, *but still hot.*

Stay focused, Maggie. Don't let him get inside your head.

"Thank you," I said casually. We sat down on the couch with about 3 feet in between us.

He took a deep breath.

"I need to know more about you," he abruptly blurted out. "Give me the whole story of Maggie the Great."

"The whole story, huh?"

The string lights, the jacket around my shoulders, the questions…all of this was starting to feel like I was on an episode of The Bachelor and competing for the first impression rose.

"Well, I'm the youngest of three siblings. My parents got divorced when I was 15. I'm studying Hospitality Management at Michigan State University…Um, I love dogs…"

"Jesus," he interrupted me, laughing. "You'd write a terrible autobiography, my dear."

I joined in his laughter.

"Sorry. I just don't really talk about myself much. Nothing too interesting has happened to me."

"You stayed in a foreign country, alone, and you ended up living with a family of hooligans on a vineyard in rural Italy. I'd say you've done some pretty interesting things."

"Fair point, but this is one of the most reckless and spontaneous decisions I've ever made. I normally can't decide what I want to save my life. This time was different for some reason. I just really wanted to stay...so I did. It felt good to just do what I wanted for once."

"Such spontaneity wasn't because of a cute boy you met the night before and hoped to bump into again...was it?"

"I did meet a boy...I don't recall him being cute though."

He gasped dramatically. "I have a fragile ego, Miss Maggie. Don't hurt me like that."

Before I could even respond, his expression changed to dead serious, and he slid closer to me.

"Don't even try to tell me that you don't feel what I feel. I won't let you. My family won't care. None of them even have to know."

Did he just say he won't let me?

He was inching closer to me as he spoke. It was actually kind of intimidating. I almost felt like I was being yelled at. Of course, he had consumed a lot of alcohol so I was pretty sure this behavior was just a result of that. Still, it made me skittish.

"August, relax." I put my hand on his chest. His eyes never leaving mine, he slowly placed his right hand on mine. Before I could get in another word, I saw his lips inching closer and closer to mine.

I had to move or stop him somehow.

But I really didn't want to.

He paused just before our lips touched. There was that consent thing again. I could feel him waiting for me to approve.

I pulled back slightly and dropped my head; his lips unintentionally met my forehead. He didn't pull away though.

"I can wait...until you're ready," he whispered against my skin. "But I won't quit trying, Maggie. I've got some big plans for us."

Us.

Holy shit. Hearing that come out of his mouth made me almost give in right then and there. How could I, or anyone, refuse this man? Besides being a bit...overly passionate at times, he was perfect. I felt proud of myself for not kissing him, but, at the same time, I was regretting my decision to play it safe.

I smiled shyly at him, unsure of how to reply to that very...forward comment.

I took his hand in mine and stood up. We headed back inside without saying another word.

Fran and Leone had already gone to bed, and Bel was laying on the couch watching Netflix on her phone. Remnants of the evening's celebration lingered on the floor; the streamers hung sadly in the glow of the living room lamp.

I walked with August to the bottom of the staircase.

"Was this a better prom for you?"

"It was. Thank you. I had a lot of fun."

He smiled, but I could see the defeat in his eyes. I wished I could tell him about what Bel had said. I wished we could go upstairs and talk more in his room. If only he knew it wasn't about him but, instead, about me having integrity for once in my damn life. This is

Bel's house and her family, and if it was so important to her that I not get involved with her brothers that she would actually tell me not to do it, then the least I can do is honor her wishes.

"I think I'm going to stay down here and hang out with Bel for a bit." I figured it was safer to be down here with Bel than upstairs all alone with August.

He lingered for a moment, gazing at my lips like he was hungry for them. Then, he turned around and headed up the stairs in silence.

I poked my head into the living room and waved at Bel to let her know I was down here. She waved back and then returned to her show.

I reentered the kitchen. The sink was full of dishes, and most of the counter space was taken up with dirty pots and pans. I started grabbing glasses and dessert plates and placing them in the dishwasher.

"Hey, Maggie! Don't do those dishes; it's August's turn tonight." Bel shouted from the living room.

"It's okay. I got it!"

While I was standing at the sink , I heard a thump outside the kitchen window. I thought about going to get Bel to investigate with me, but I didn't want to bug her again. Besides, I am an independent woman, after all.

I stepped outside through the side door and cautiously peeked around the corner of the house. I gasped way more loudly than I should've when I saw a man slumped against the side of the house.

I squinted to try and see who the dark figure was. As I got closer,

I realized it was Nic. Drunk beyond words.

"Nic? What the hell are you doing out here?"

He didn't even flinch or look to see who was talking to him.

"How about you go back in the house and fetch me another beer." He was waving his hand toward the door.

"Excuse me? I'm not a waitress. Get up and come inside. Your mom will be furious if she sees you like this."

"Like you know anything about me or my mom. Just leave me alone, Margaret."

Now I was pissed. Obviously I didn't know them that well, but I thought of myself as a step above a random stranger. Hell, I was just in their family photos. And Margaret, really?

"It's Maggie, not Margaret. You can literally get every other fact wrong about me for the rest of my time here, but just remember that one. Please."

His eyes widened at my unexpected bluntness. I was never this direct, except when it came to one thing...my name.

He had a puzzled look on his face like he was trying to figure out who this new Maggie was and why she was giving him such a hard time. He definitely didn't seem used to having people talk back to him.

Before he could even try to spit out another rude comment, I reached out to help him stand up.

"You can be drunk and rude inside. Come on, let's go."

He looked at me, eyes narrowed.

He finally stood up without taking my hand and followed me to the side door. I held it open for him, and he gave me a dirty look before taking a wobbly step forward. I may have karma to thank for what happened next. Nic tripped over his untied shoelace as he stepped into the kitchen and landed on the floor in a heap. I had to bite my tongue from laughing so hard.

He stood up, trying to pretend like nothing had happened, then stumbled to the staircase. Bel must have been blasting her movie in her headphones because she, apparently, didn't even hear my grand entrance with Bigfoot.

I honestly didn't know why I was helping him, but I continued to follow him all the way up the stairs. Not that I would've been able to do anything if he fell backwards on me except get crushed; he's a whole foot taller than me.

Anyway, I was just basically trying to be the bigger person at this point and help him get to bed. At the same time, I had to admit that his little tumble had definitely been the high point of my night.

But I was so curious. Where did he go when he disappeared? We were supposed to be quarantined so I doubted that Fran and Leone were letting him actually go anywhere. And why was he so drunk? From what I could see, his life was hardly a struggle. He had a loving family and a beautiful home. He worked every day at something he loved. Who could have issues with an arrangement like that?

As I passed August's room, I leaned my right shoulder against the partially open door. The creaking caused him to shift and roll over so that I could see his face.

There I was, staring at him again.

His hair lay flatter than usual. He tucked his two hands under his chin like a little kid would and then took a deep breath.

When he wasn't being brash, August had a calming effect on me. He was an open book. I knew exactly how he felt at all times. But Nic...being around Nic just made me feel confused and overwhelmed. Like now, hearing him huffing and puffing in his room.

I headed there to make sure he didn't need anything else and was met with the door being shut in my face.

Again.

I caught it just before it slammed, then entered Nic's room and shut the door quickly and quietly behind me. "What the hell is your problem?" I was whispering so I didn't wake August. Hearing that come out of my mouth was shocking. I hated being confrontational; it felt so unnatural to me. I blamed that on my parents who never confronted me about anything.

This may sound strange, but sometimes, in middle school and high school, I actually wanted to be yelled at, disciplined like my other friends. I just wanted my parents to notice me, even if it was for fucking something up. My parents were always so caught up in all their drama that I always felt like it didn't really matter what I did.

Nic glared at me while taking off his black Adidas sweatshirt. He was shirtless now. Why did he feel comfortable enough to do that in front of me?

I avoided looking anywhere other than his eyes. His deep, dark brown eyes that were filled with angst. I gestured with a small head shake, as if to say, "Well? Nothing to say?"

"You've been here what? A week? And you think you can boss

me around?"

He took a large step toward me. I stood my ground. I felt the heat of his breath, and the smell of liquor nearly knocked me over.

"Nic, I have zero interest in bossing you or anyone around. Believe it or not, tonight I was just trying to help. You were in pretty bad shape out there."

He was quiet for about 30 seconds, hands on hips, his weight on his left leg, swaying slightly.

Looking down, he finally said, "You know, she has a habit of taking in strays like you. And then everything goes to shit. You shouldn't be here."

I felt like he had just slapped me across the face.

Before he could get another word out, I turned and walked calmly out of the room, shutting his door quietly behind me. No amount of wine could make me confrontational enough to reply to such harsh words.

I could feel the tears coming. So much for trying to help.

Maybe he was right. Maybe the others were just trying to be polite by not asking me to leave. I had started to get too comfortable with the arrangement, with the feeling of family, but I wasn't family.

I needed to go. It was time. The whole situation was getting out of control. There was no way I could stay here after hearing how Nic felt about me.

Why couldn't Fran have had 3 daughters instead?

First thing in the morning, I'll call for a taxi into the city. I'll get coffee somewhere and use their WiFi to find a hotel that's still open.

I've felt invisible for too long to think that I finally deserved the space, the family now. I fell into my bed, drunk and angry. I didn't even have the energy to take off my makeup or brush my teeth.

All I could do as I lay there in pitch darkness was cry softly and try to figure out how to leave tomorrow morning without waking Bel.

I reached up and knocked incredibly softly on the wall one time. I waited, hopeful for a sign that maybe leaving was a mistake. That there was something worth sticking around for.

But everything was silent, and no knock came from the other side. A single tear rolled down my cheek as I drifted off to sleep.

CHAPTER SEVEN

I woke up and rubbed my eyes before moving my fingertips up to my temples, working in small circles as my wine hangover headache worsened by the second. I slowly rolled over to check my phone, hoping I still had enough time to escape. I closed my eyes as I remembered my horrible conversation with Nic last night.

It was 5:47am, and I wasn't sure what time Fran and Leone woke up so I figured now was my best shot at getting out without having to explain to anyone why I was leaving. I didn't want to get Nic in trouble even if his words hurt me in a way I couldn't quite explain.

I headed to the bathroom where I brushed my teeth and grabbed all my stuff.

Carefully placing all my clothes and toiletries into my suitcase and unplugging my phone charger from the outlet, I tried my best not to wake Bel.

I knew she was going to be upset with me; I could tell how much she was enjoying having an older sister figure around the house. She had already told me of her grand plans to give me makeovers and show me the best shops around town when quarantine ended. No matter what Nic had said, I knew Bel did not want me to leave.

I felt like I was letting her down, but I had to do this. It just wasn't worth it. I ripped a piece of paper out of my notebook and scribbled down a note to her.

Bel, please don't be mad. Trust that this is for the best and has nothing to do with you. I've loved being your roommate. I'll see you soon (come visit me - Michigan will be waiting for you). Love, Maggie.

I tucked the note slightly under my pillow so that she wouldn't see it immediately. I wanted her to find it eventually, not the exact moment she opened her eyes. I waved sadly to her side of the room before heading quietly down the stairs with my luggage. I'd only known her for a week, but I could already feel myself missing her.

As I came down the stairs, I was glad to see that the kitchen was dim.

I passed through and was about two steps away from the side door, my escape route, when I heard, "Going somewhere?" from an achingly familiar voice.

I jumped about 5 feet in the air.

"Jesus Christ, Nic?! I caught my breath. Why...the hell...are you just sitting there in the dark?"

"I couldn't sleep. I came down for a snack."

He was eyeing my bags. "So...you're taking off?"

I looked at him like he had three heads.

"Yeah...I...I just think it's best. I mean...after all you said last night. It was...an unexpected...um...perspective. I...should never have expected so much from your mom, I mean, she was just so kind, and I...I... didn't know how to say no..."

This wasn't going well. I was literally just sputtering, trying to put together a fucking sentence.

Nic watched me intently with his typical brooding stare.

I took a deep breath during which I decided to just be honest with him. I would probably never see him again anyway. I took a small step toward him.

"Actually...you know what, Nic? Your perspective last night wasn't just...unexpected. It was also pretty hurtful to me. I'm truly sorry that you feel like everything has gone to shit since I got here because I've been purposefully trying to be as useful...to everyone...as I possibly can. And I'm sorry you don't like me...but...I'm...not a terrible person. Lots of people think I'm a pretty decent friend. But anyway, you made it very clear how you felt...so...I'm going to go now."

I grabbed the handle of my suitcase and turned toward the door.

"Please don't."

What the hell?

"I was a complete ass last night...you didn't deserve any of that." Nic was looking at me with an expression I had never seen before on his face. He literally looked like a different person.

Part of me wanted to keep walking out the door, and the other part wanted to stay exactly where I was.

What the hell is going on right now, and who is this person?

Nic stood up.

God, he's tall. Somehow taller than August, I think.

"I don't want you to go. Last night, I was just trying to make you feel bad because you were making so much sense."

I was looking at him like he had three heads again.

I suddenly realized we had been staring at each other for way too long so I shifted my gaze which then landed on his torso. At that point, I just looked down.

I could feel him still looking at me. Finally, he broke the silence.

"Can I show you something?"

"What?"

"Follow me." He pushed past me as he headed out the side door, not even looking to see if I was following him.

"Wait!" I called out. "Let me go put my suitcase and backpack away."

He nodded and folded his arms. "Go ahead, but hurry. We don't have much time. I'll wait."

Don't have much time? For what?

I ran back into the house, pulled my luggage up the stairs, and quietly placed my suitcase at the foot of my bed where it normally sat. I opened it and unfolded a few shirts so it didn't look packed, then threw my backpack on my bed. I looked to make sure Bel was still sleeping before heading back outside to meet Nic.

Once he saw me exit the side door, he started heading for the barns. I had no idea why he was taking me out there, but, for some reason, I felt completely at peace following him.

Each barn had its own name written in cursive lettering above the entrance. The one we were approaching was called "Lillian," which I assumed was a family name, maybe Fran's mother. It was a creamy off-white color and had a grey metal roof. The smallest barn, which was a pale pink color, was labelled "Bella," named after Bel of course.

Nic opened the unlocked door and flicked on the lights. It was very bohemian looking inside. Beaded, sparkling chandeliers hung sporadically from the vaulted ceiling. There were rows of dark, wooden benches adorned with eccentric, colorful cushions. The aisle was lined with lanterns. A copper arch wrapped in greenery stood near the front of the barn and there were a few elegant watercolor paintings hung up on the walls. I would pay good money to have my wedding ceremony in a place this beautiful.

"Sit here" Nic said, almost shyly, grabbing a chair and placing it directly opposite a large, multicolored stained glass window on the back wall that depicted a garden scene with poppies, lilies, sunflowers, and wisteria.

I sat, obeying his order.

"It's so pretty."

"Just wait." Nic started pacing back and forth behind me like a caged animal, staring at his phone.

Maybe he brought me out here so nobody would hear him killing me. He cleared his throat.

"Are you ready?"

"Ready for what?" Nic jogged over to the door and turned off the lights.

"Um...hello?" Okay, this was it. I was going to die in a barn named Lillian.

"Just give it a second."

We waited in silence for...it.

Was he getting ready to propose?

Just as I started to say, "Nic, what the hell," the sun, having just then cleared the trees, suddenly shone so brightly through that stained glass. It created this rainbow beam of light from the window all the way to the other side of the barn.

I gasped and then just sat there with my mouth open.

It was exquisitely beautiful.

After about three minutes, Nic broke the quiet.

"It's beautiful, no?"

I nodded.

He brought another chair over and sat next to me. He leaned back, stretching his long legs in front of him. His face looked so different now to me. Every other time I had been this close to Nic, he was either unhappy or angry or covered in sweat. I realized that this was the first time I had seen him relaxed.

He was much tanner than August and Bel from working at the vineyard full-time. I had never noticed how gorgeous his eyes were. They're a deep green on the outer rim and grow into a hazel near the middle.

"She thought so too. She loved sunrises. She always said they were the only thing we could count on each day. The thing that always promised us a new beginning, free from the burdens of all our yesterdays." He spoke calmly and evenly.

"Who's she?"

"Ellie. She collected them, sunrises, like little kids collect lighting bugs or trading cards, that sort of thing."

"Was Ellie a philosopher? Sounds deep."

His face remained serious.

"Ellie was American, like you. She was from Virginia, studying in Florence for 6 months."

I sat up in my chair. Whatever this was, I could sense it was important to him.

"This was about a year ago. Jack, Elliott and I went to the beach one Saturday to go surfing. We hated the tourists who just took over the sand and the water, especially on weekends, but it was the off-season and a pretty overcast day so we thought our odds would be good." I met his eyes briefly before he looked down at his clasped hands again.

"We were there pretty much all day, but, after surfing for a few hours, we were all so tired that we passed out on the sand. Not our smartest move considering all our phones and wallets were just laying out around us. I woke up first; there was this group of American girls who had set up right next to us. I just rolled my eyes and lay back down. I was nearly asleep again when one of them approached us, asking if I could take their picture. What I soon found out was that she really wanted me to take hundreds of pictures because every time I took one, she would say, "It's not quite right." It was really annoying. But Ellie was hilarious."

He took a deep breath.

"In every picture I took, she made the goofiest faces, like she didn't really care how she looked. I loved it. We stayed there until it got dark, all of us sharing stories and drinking lots and lots of wine.

Ellie and I took a walk down the beach and ended up walking for hours and just talking about everything you could possibly imagine."

I had no idea why he was telling me all of this, but I was starting to get a bit worried about where it was leading.

"She just checked every box for me. When we got back to the others, they were all asleep. So then I had the brilliant idea: to invite her to come stay at the vineyard for the weekend. You should've seen mom's face when I showed up about three in the morning with this random girl."

I was no longer as pained by the memory of Nic and my conversation last night. The way he was talking to me now made it seem like he actually liked me.

"We spent the rest of her time abroad together, whether it was at the beach or here at the vineyard. We couldn't get enough of each other. On her last day here, she wanted to see one last sunrise together. I told her to meet me here at dawn, at the very window you're sitting at, because, as you can see, it's the most beautiful sunrise in the world. I had discovered it just a few days before. I knew that the stained glass window in Lillian faced east, so I woke up early and came out here to check it out. As soon as I saw it, I couldn't wait to show her."

"I couldn't sleep that last night...knowing it would be our last sunrise, knowing I may never see her again. I just had to make it extra special. I set it up perfectly with her favorite breakfast, fruit and yogurt, I had flowers, the whole show."

"Thoughtful," I muttered under my breath.

"So..." He took a deep breath. "I waited and waited for Ellie, but she didn't show up and she wasn't answering her phone, so I tried to call one of her friends. Just then I got a call."

My heart dropped. I didn't even know this girl, or Nic really, but I was invested in his story and was now fearful for the end.

"It was the hospital. They said that Ellie had been in an accident. They had seen a lot of texts from me on her phone so that's why they contacted me."

My shoulders sank lower. I couldn't look away from him.

"She um...had a collapsed lung and she broke four ribs...and then... they found a bleed in her brain. She didn't stand a chance." He hesitated and I could see the sheer pain in his eyes.

"She deserved a chance, Maggie."

I had only dealt with death on one occasion thus far in my life, and that was

Gram, my best friend. She had breast cancer, on and off for years, so we saw her death coming. We were prepared. I couldn't even begin to imagine the pain of losing someone you love in a split second, especially when they were on their way to see you.

"I'm the reason she got in that taxi that morning. I'm the reason she didn't get that last sunrise." His voice was shaking now. I placed my hand gently on top of his, hoping this gesture was not overstepping but rather comforting to him.

"I'm so sorry," was all I could get out.

He had a hard time looking at me. "Thank you." I didn't remove my hand just yet.

"Maggie, I've been...awful to you. I'm sorry. I've been a total mess since she died, wishing it had been me in that taxi instead of her. And then you showed up, and...I don't know...I've been wanting other people to hurt like me. I know that's not right. I'm sorry."

It all made sense now: the anger, the frustration, the pushing everyone away. The "issues" that Bel had mentioned. He was grieving. And grief could make you do things you didn't know you were capable of. When Gram died, I didn't want to leave her house. I think I spent a whole month either in her house or alone in my room. I wouldn't talk to anyone because I knew nobody really understood.

"I'm still figuring this all out, and each day is a struggle, but I promise not to take it out on you anymore."

We sat in silence for what felt like an hour before he stood, reaching out both hands to help me up.

We stood and both took a collective deep breath.

"We want you here, Maggie. All of us."

It was as if I had completely forgotten I had been planning to leave in the first place.

I looked at him, feeling as if I'd looked at him a thousand times before, like he was an old friend. "Nic, I'm not going anywhere."

CHAPTER EIGHT

Nic and I made our way up to the house, walking silently the entire way back. I think we were both still processing our sudden intimacy. It felt like we had skipped a handful of steps to get to this point in our friendship, bypassing the awkwardness and fear of being vulnerable. I'm not complaining, though. Especially given the previous state of our relationship.

Neither of us realized how long we'd been gone. When we entered the house, the whole family was seated around the table, passing scrambled eggs and bacon around and laughing. All of which came to a sudden halt when we entered, together, from outside.

August, unsurprisingly, was the first to question us.

"What were you guys doing out there?" He looked extremely suspicious.

It was a fair question. Nic and I hadn't demonstrated even the slightest bit of closeness since I'd been here. It did seem somewhat strange for us to be hanging out alone first thing in the morning.

Nic didn't hesitate for a second. "The American here was worried sick that she was messing up home base. We were both up early so she asked if I could give her a little extra assistance before Mom woke up." Fran looked confused. I'm sure she was wondering why I hadn't just asked her for help.

I wasn't exactly sure why a lie was necessary. It wasn't like we had done anything wrong. But if that was the story he needed to go with, I was willing to play along.

Bel caught my eye from across the room and nonchalantly held up the folded note I'd left for her on my bed earlier this morning.

She quietly put it back in her shirt pocket and, thankfully, didn't say anything about it to the rest of the family.

August's brow was furrowed. He was clearly not happy with me spending alone time with his brother.

Fran approached me, coffee mug in hand.

"Sweetie, you should've just told me you needed a hand out there. I would've been more than glad to walk you through things again. Don't feel like you can't come to me; I've got your back." She kissed my cheek and passed off the coffee.

I was always a bit thrown off by Fran's kindness and willingness to help me. I'd grown up having to figure most things out for myself. Gram was luckily around for the important stuff like the specific joys of growing up as a female, but, when she passed, I lost the one person who really showed me that she cared about me, didn't just say it to say it. She loved my brothers and her other grandchildren just as much, but we had a special connection...a bond.

Fran reminds me of her. I'm starting to feel like part of this family, and I know it's only temporary, but it still feels really good.

"I'm sorry, Fran. I just didn't want to bother you again when you'd already taken so much time showing me everything. I hope it's okay that I asked Nic. He was up early with me, and he's got so much experience working here, so I just figured he would be a good person to ask."

I'm pretty good at this acting thing. Do I call Hollywood or do they call me?

"Of course," she said.

I was seated next to August when Nic ran upstairs to his room. That was the last I would see of him for the day. Probably best; this morning was intense.

"So you and Nic were up early together?" It seemed like he was trying to sound playful but wasn't quite pulling it off. It made me very uneasy. Despite going along with Nic's lie, I wasn't hiding anything from August, not that it would matter if I was. I didn't owe him anything.

"It was unintentional, really. I woke up early and couldn't get back to sleep so I just decided to get up. When I went downstairs, he was sitting down there. It was the perfect opportunity to ask for some tips."

"You know, you could've asked me for help."

"I know that...I just didn't want to ruin our time out on the patio with work-related issues."

"So you...enjoyed our time on the patio?" He immediately dropped the conversation about Nic.

"I thought I made that clear, no?"

"Not exactly. You seemed nervous." He casually squeezed my upper thigh under the table. This was the first time he had touched me without my consent. Not that it really bothered me, but I could tell he was getting more confident.

"Do I make you nervous, Maggie?" He squeezed tighter. I brushed his wandering hand off my leg.

"Don't flatter yourself. I just take a little bit of time to get comfortable, that's all. And I'm not used to being around family that's close like this."

He grabbed a piece of bread and slid it in his mouth as he rose from his seat.

"You're going to tell me more about this not-so-close family of yours today as we paint the new shed." He signaled for me to stand and join him.

"I'm supposed to be working with Nic today."

His eyes lit up like he'd just been given a challenge.

"Hey mom!" Fran whipped her head around as she wiped the counter.

"There was a mistake on the schedule today." He nudged my arm and started heading for the door. "Maggie is working with me on painting today." He winked at me.

He swung the door open and let me go through first. I felt rude for leaving without even waiting for Fran's reply.

I heard Fran's loud protest: "The schedule's perfect!"

"She already suffered this morning with Nic; she needs a rest. I'll take care of her. I'll even fix the schedule!" He shouted the last part as he moved through the doorway.

Fran was not about to try to change August's mind. "Fine...but I better see more painting than talking! Have fun!" She yelled this through the closed door.

August joined me outside and directed me to the shed we'd be painting. It was currently a dull beige color. He told me that we'd be painting it bright white because that's what resonated with brides and made them more excited about the venue.

"What about you? Does it make you excited, Ms. Maggie?"

I laughed and shook my head. "Are you asking me to marry you, August?"

He smiled boldly. "What if I was?"

I smiled shyly while picking up a paintbrush. I opened up a can of the most perfectly white shade of white, and got to work.

August asked me tons of questions as we painted. But not in an annoying way. I just still had to get used to how much he wanted to know about me. Frankly, I wasn't used to men showing that much interest in my life. I had just recently gotten out of a relationship where I could've dyed my hair bright purple on a trip to the bathroom, and I guarantee he wouldn't have noticed when I got back.

After an hour or so, we took a break and sat propped against the shed gulping water.

"So Ms. Maggie, the real question is: how is a beautiful girl like you still single?"

Um...*still?* Jesus, I'm only twenty-one.

Regardless, it was happening. We were doing the cliche flirting thing again, I guess. I was flattered, but I didn't know how to play it.

While I couldn't really fight my physical attraction to him, I kept reminding myself that this relationship would upset Bel, and probably the rest of the family. I also knew a fling within the household while all of us were stuck in quarantine was the worst idea ever. If we were going to do this, it had to be a covert operation. Like, I'm talking CIA classified level secrecy.

"I don't really know. I just can't seem to find a good guy out there. Starting to believe they're a myth, you know, like unicorns and fairies."

He quickly perked up from his slumped position.

"They're not a myth. I'm half unicorn and half fairy." He said this with a completely straight face.

I couldn't help but burst into laughter.

"You're ridiculous is what you are."

"Ridiculously into you." He turned and faced me completely now. He was always so damn forward. He just says what he feels and goes recklessly after what he wants. I love it. I could feel my apprehension starting to disintegrate.

"You are persistent, I'll give you that."

"I think that's a compliment?"

"It is." I smiled without making eye contact.

"Maggie…"

Uh oh.

"Yes?" I inched my body ever so slightly to face him. It would've been rude not to, right?

"You want to know why you're single?"

"Oh, yes. Please enlighten me."

He grinned. "You're single because your standards are high. As they should be. You know what you want. You don't settle. I can see it in you, and that's why you're apprehensive about me. You're intrigued, but you're unsure of my intentions so you're holding back."

He wasn't wrong.

"I'm not going to hurt you, Maggie. My intentions are good."

"I'm not afraid you're going to hurt me."

"Then what are you afraid of?"

That was a good question. Was my anxiety all about keeping my promise to Bel? Would Fran and Leone really be upset? Was I actually unsure about him?

"I'm not sure," I said quietly.

"Be selfish. For once in your goddamn life, Maggie. You're always so worried about everyone else. Do something that makes you feel good." His face was inches from mine.

A flood of courage overtook me, and I leaned in hastily and kissed him. I thought I would feel regret when my lips finally touched his, but I felt nothing but heat.

We didn't skip a beat. Our bodies quickly became entangled. His hands ran through my hair and then made their way down my back. I pulled back slightly and opened my eyes. He smiled down at me as we held each other tightly for a minute or two.

That is, until we heard Fran calling us for dinner. By design, we were on the side of the shed opposite to the house so nobody could've seen us, but still, we were going to have to be really careful if this happened again.

It better happen again.

As I took a step toward the house, my arm was suddenly jolted backwards and, without even a millisecond of hesitation, August was kissing me again, and I was kissing him back. He wrapped his hands around my waist and kissed me more slowly this time.

I felt like I was the only girl he'd ever kissed, like he had waited and carefully crafted this kiss just for me. I hated how complicated this would make things, and I hated that I would have to lie to Bel or seriously disappoint her, but I definitely didn't hate how this beautiful, tall, strong man was making me feel things I hadn't felt in a long time. Making me feel seen. I'd kissed a dozen or so decently attractive men before, but none of them were August. None of them felt like this.

He pulled away, brushing my hair out of my face. "How does being selfish feel?"

I looked down at my paint-splattered feet, blushing. "Overdue," I whispered.

He took my chin in his hand, raising it slightly before kissing me one last time. It was short and soft, and I didn't want it to end.

He squeezed my hand once and released it as we walked toward the house for dinner, both knowing without a word that we weren't going to tell a soul what had just happened. Also knowing it probably wasn't the last time it was going to happen.

That night when I got into bed, I heard a soft knock on the wall right next to my head. I reached up, hoping Bel hadn't heard it. She looked asleep from where I was, but as soon as I knocked back, her head perked up, and she rolled over.

"What's with the knocking? Is there an animal stuck in the wall, or are you secretly communicating with my brother?"

"What are you talking about? I didn't hear any knocking." I decided playing dumb was the only route here.

"Well, let's just say I've never hoped for a creature to be living in my wall more than right now." She rolled her eyes. I didn't know how to respond to this. It sounded like she had a hunch about me and August and was testing me, but I couldn't be sure.

Bel sat up and crossed her legs.

"Since we're both awake, let's chat." She waved the note I had written her this morning in the air.

Ugh. I completely forgot about that stupid note. "Bel, I'm sorry. It was a mistake."

"You were seriously going to leave without saying goodbye? You thought a little scribbled handwritten note was enough? Do I mean that little to you?"

Bel didn't show many emotions, and she was normally extremely chill. This had really hurt her. I felt like absolute shit.

"I know. It was stupid, and I was being a coward, and frankly, I knew if I had to talk to you about it, that I probably wouldn't go through with it. I am so so sorry, Bel. I fucked up. I just felt like I didn't have a choice.

She was glaring at me.

Okay, here goes. I took a deep breath, preparing to out Nic.

"Some things were said. It was communicated to me that I didn't belong here and that I needed to leave."

"By who?"

I should have gone through with it. She deserved the truth from me after what I had done. But then she would go and yell at Nic for driving me away, and it would cause more problems. I had forgiven Nic for what he'd said. I definitely didn't want to relive it now. I took a deep breath.

"My parents. On the phone. They yelled at me and told me how irresponsible I was being and how I was taking advantage of your family. It really messed me up mentally. I just thought I was doing everyone a favor by going."

Her face shifted from frustrated to empathetic.

"I'm sorry they said that, Maggie. They clearly don't understand how much we all like you being here. You fit in so well with us. I'm starting to forget what it was like without you."

I smiled and walked over to sit on her bed next to her.

"Thanks, Bel. I promise not to try and leave again. I should've just talked to you about it. I really am sorry. I'm so happy to be here."

She picked up the note, ripped it into a bunch of tiny pieces, and then looked at me sternly.

I smiled and grabbed her for a big bear hug; she fought me at first but quickly gave in. Pretty soon, we were rolling around on her bed and laughing hysterically.

After we had both settled in bed, I turned to face the wall, imagining August lying there on the other side. I wanted so badly to knock. But after what Bel and I had just gone through, plus her "creature in the wall" comment, I decided to just close my eyes.

CHAPTER NINE

I'd been living with the Costelli's for three weeks, and sometimes I actually forgot that we were even in quarantine at all. If I had been stuck in my father's minuscule condo this entire time, rather than at this beautiful Italian vineyard, with a beautiful Italian man, quarantine would have been much, much more difficult.

That first kiss with August was quickly followed by many more. We basically couldn't keep our hands off each other. Any time I saw him, I found myself craving his touch and longing for our next passionate moment. Our daily mission was just to be alone and close as much as possible.

None of the family knew, at least that we were aware of, and we were trying our absolute hardest to keep it that way. It wasn't easy. And August often made it exceptionally difficult by doing things like slipping his hand in between my legs at the dinner table and "accidentally" closing the door behind me when I entered his room to "tell him something."

The rest of the family was bound to find out. It just seemed inevitable. Part of me wanted them to find out. I mean, this was stressful. Fun as hell...but still very stressful. And lying to everyone definitely didn't feel good...but, oh my god, the way August made me feel, that rush when he grabbed me...I literally couldn't say no. How did everything get so complicated?

The knocking had become our thing. Every night before we fell asleep, we exchanged knocks, sometimes more than one. We had done an experiment and discovered that we could hear even super quiet ones. That came in handy when Bel didn't have her headphones on, which was basically never.

I loved hearing that knock. Knowing he was there, right on the other side of the wall, gave me such peace. I knew I was the very last thing he thought of before he went to sleep. Tell me that's not a turn-on.

Nic was now sometimes eating dinner with the family. This made me really happy. And I know it made Fran happy because, whenever he was around, she would grab his face and kiss him on the cheek or the forehead.

He had this dry sense of humor that I only discovered once he started eating with us. And he's really smart. He and Bel would have these hilarious discussions, sometimes in Italian, which I loved even though I only understood a word or phrase here and there.

August was the only one who didn't seem thrilled that Nic was spending more time with the family. It took me a while to notice, but he would just get kind of sullen at the table, especially if Nic was talking.

Nic still usually went "running" after dinner. Despite the fact that

I now considered us friends, he was still somewhat mysterious to me. He was like an onion. Layer after layer.

One night, after August and my knocks had wrapped up, and I could tell he had fallen asleep, I wandered downstairs for a glass of water. My craving for cold water turned into a craving for pasta once I opened the fridge and saw the leftovers from dinner.

I grabbed the container of penne alla vodka that Fran had spent hours making yesterday. When I shut the fridge, I saw someone standing in the doorway and let out a yelp.

The figure came into the light. Of course it was Nic. He was the only one who was ever up as late as me.

"Hey Mags, second dinner?"

I laughed. "I'd rather call it a late night snack. I couldn't sleep."

"Yeah, thinking about that pasta keeps me awake too. Mom outdid herself. You know, she normally doesn't cook such elaborate dishes; she's definitely been showing off for you."

He sat down at the counter and watched me eat a massive bite straight from the container. With pasta sauce dribbling down my chin, I shot him a "Can I help you?" look.

"Mags, where've you been recently? It seems like you're always out and about, which is weird considering we're quarantined in the same house."

Why did he keep calling me Mags? He'd never done that before.

I took a napkin from the stack on the counter and wiped my chin.

I wasn't sure how I felt hearing him call me Mags. It seemed like something my parents should have done when I was growing up, but just forgot to do, among many other things. I was always just Maggie or Magnolia.

"I've been here, weirdo. I sleep like 10 steps away from you every single night. You're the one who's always going out late for "jogs" or whatever it is you do out there in the dark." I raised my eyebrows, insinuating dramatically that he was up to no good.

"Hey, I gotta get out of the house somehow. If I didn't, I'd be getting sick of you all a lot quicker than I already am." He sat down next to me at the counter.

I was still thinking about the jogging. Where the hell did he go every night? Doing laps around the vineyard had to get old at some point.

I really never understood people who ran, for fun that is. Of course I understood it when people were running away from kidnappers or zombies. But I made it a strict point to not be friends with anyone who saw running as a fun activity.

"Where do you even go on these runs?"

He looked at me and smiled. I figured he was basking in the thought that I was concerned enough to ask about where he went or what he did.

"Come on, I'll show you." He patted my back, which felt friendly enough, but still took me by surprise.

Here we go again.

Why was he always carting me off to unknown destinations? Would it kill him to just tell me where we were going for once, or even ask if I wanted to go with him in the first place?

I watched him walk to the door without budging from my seat.

"You know, you could ask if I'd like to come with you rather than just bossing me around and expecting that I'll come wherever and whenever you say. Especially if running is involved. I don't run. I refuse, Nic." I crossed my arms in protest.

He grinned, not quite fully smiling. "I like when you fight back, but trust me on this one. No running involved."

I rolled my eyes, a gesture he often elicited from me.

I was slightly concerned that August would find out about my little jaunts with Nic and be jealous. He was definitely asleep upstairs, but if he happened to wake up and knock, only to find that I was MIA and with Nic, he would not be pleased.

August was very protective in general. He always lost his temper hearing about the awful ways men have treated me in the past. It was endearing but sometimes scary how upset he got. I could only imagine how angry he'd be if he thought Nic, his own brother, and I were doing anything other than talking as friends.

But the point was we weren't. Of course we weren't. And there was absolutely nothing wrong with me being friends with his brother.

You know what? I don't want to miss out on something perfectly respectable and potentially really cool just because it may unreasonably freak out my boyfriend.

"Sure, why not. No running!"

Before we left, we grabbed hoodies and flashlights from the mud room. Nic also took a bandana.

The vineyard had a thick patch of woods behind the barns, but I'd never been back that far. As we headed in that direction, I looked up at the almost-full moon and then over at Nic. He had the same peaceful expression on his face that he'd had in the barn a couple weeks ago. I liked seeing him like this.

As we entered the woods, I could see the moon peeking through the dense branches every so often. We were on some sort of path that barely looked like a path. It was so narrow that we had to walk single file. Nic moved through the thick, dark forest just like he pruned the grape vines: efficiently and effortlessly. He knew every twist and turn of that path. He even knew where there was a low-hanging branch that he held up for me. As we walked, we were completely silent. I inhaled deeply; the aroma was intoxicating.

Nic suddenly stopped and turned to me. "Okay, the rest of the way you can't look."

He took the bandana out of his pocket and leaned forward a bit so he could look me in the eye.

"Trust me."

I took a breath and turned around. "Fine."

He tied the bandana around my head so that it covered my eyes.

This was the part where the girl gets murdered. I've watched enough horror movies to know how this ends.

What's that saying? Curiosity killed the stupid, naive girl?

Yeah, hello, that's me.

He had me hold on to his shoulders as he led me on. We must have gone 50 feet or so when I heard the gentle lapping sound of water and felt pebbles under my feet.

Nic removed the bandana. I was immediately calmed and enchanted by the sight revealed. We were standing on a tiny rock beach in front of a small, shimmering lake. The moon's reflection lit up the surface of the water; it bounced off the tiny ripples like a fourth of July firework.

For the first time since arriving at the vineyard, I missed home.

"How did you find this?"

Nic shrugged. "I like to explore."

I took a few steps forward and slipped off my sandals to dip my toes in the water. Nic followed my lead and removed his sneakers.

To my surprise, it wasn't as cold as I was expecting. Lake Michigan was unbearably freezing until mid-to-late summer.

"Nic, it's beautiful." My gaze remained focused on the lake.

"The other day I was pulling weeds in the garden right beneath the kitchen window, and Bel was in there talking to mom at an annoyingly loud volume, per usual. She was going on and on about lakes, which I thought was weird and random, until I realized she was talking about you and how you're from the "Great Lakes State" or whatever you call it. She was talking about how cool you made it sound, having a different lake around every turn."

It made me smile that Bel was fascinated by my stories. Michigan was and always would be home, and I jumped at every opportunity I had to share it's beauty with anyone who would listen.

My favorite thing about Michigan was it's variety. Each corner of the state offered something completely different. The West side had some beautiful beach towns like Grand Haven and Ludington, but it also had Grand Rapids, which is a booming city filled with culture.

The East side was home to the fascinating and electric city of Detroit, which had become a lot livelier and cherished over the last decade.

Then there's Northern Michigan, which was my favorite place on Earth. Once you crossed the Mackinac Bridge into the Upper Peninsula, you entered a natural paradise of waterfalls, mountains and rocky coasts. I was always going to be a Michigander. No matter how far I went, I would find my way back.

The fact that Bel thought Michigan sounded wonderful made me want to take her there and show it off to her. I knew she'd love it just as much as I do. And I couldn't imagine a better place to visit on your first trip to the US.

"So I just thought you'd like to see it. To know you have a little piece of Michigan right here in our backyard, free for you to come and see any time, Mags."

There he was with the nickname again. The more he said it, the more it was growing on me.

I pulled him in for a hug. It wasn't until his arms were wrapped tightly around my lower back that I realized we'd never hugged, or barely even touched before. It felt strange, unfamiliar, but surprisingly comfortable.

Hugging Nic was so different from hugging August who always grabbed me so tightly, like he was afraid I'd slip out of his grasp. I liked it, of course, but...sometimes I just wished he could relax. Nic's hands were gentler and didn't stray from the position they originally found.

"Thank you, Nic."

"You're welcome, Magnolia."

He remembered.

I had told him that was the one thing he needed to remember about me, and he did. I would have thought he was way too drunk that night to remember anything, let alone an important detail like that.

Did friends hug this long?

Thinking probably not, I awkwardly wriggled my way out of his grasp and then bent down to roll up my pajama bottoms. I walked a few steps into the water.

"What's the deal with your name anyway? Why were you so offended by being called Margaret? Elementary school nemesis?"

He rolled up his jeans and joined me in the water; we were standing about ankle deep at this point. It was the perfect temperature.

"You misunderstood me. I don't have a problem with the name Margaret at all; I just get frustrated when people automatically assume that's what Maggie is short for. My full name is too important to just be overlooked like that."

I always maintained a dead serious expression when I talked about my name to let people know right away that it was very special to me and not a trivial matter. I could get pretty judg-ey with people who made light of it.

We stood there staring at each other for a couple seconds. It wasn't that I didn't want to tell him; I was just rarely asked about it. And when I did talk about it, I usually ended up crying.

His expression matched mine. "So...are you going to tell me about it?"

I took a deep breath.

"My grandmother — my mom's mom — we were incredibly close. She was more of a mother to me than my own mom. She was just this amazing woman. So giving, so loving, hilariously funny, smart as a whip. I trusted her with my life, my secrets, everything. We talked about boys and all the other stuff that girls usually talked about with their moms. I was named Magnolia after her."

Nic's face seemed to flood with concern.

"When she died, I knew I had to do something special to commemorate her. She deserved a remembrance that was strong and graceful and beautiful, just like she was. And I wanted it to be some place close by so I could still talk to her whenever I needed to. I know that's silly. But I just couldn't imagine not being able to tell her about all my drama anymore. So I saved all my money for a year and then, with my dad's help, planted the most beautiful magnolia tree you could ever imagine in our backyard. My mom didn't really understand the gesture, but that made sense because she never seemed to understand anything about Gram."

What I didn't tell him was that, after Gram died, I discovered that mom had been stealing money from her, and because Gram was so generous and loving and trusting, she never knew. My mom barely flinched when Gram died. All she was to her was an easy mark. I wouldn't let her ruin this story, though.

I smiled, pausing to remember how amazing that tree looked when it bloomed for the first time. My bedroom window had a clear view of it, and I looked at it every single day, feeling like every tiny, new blossom was Gram stopping by and checking on me.

"The tree only seemed fitting, you know, our name and all. That tree became my favorite spot in the world. Sometimes, my parents would literally have to pull me inside for dinner or bed or whatever because I refused to come out from underneath it. I can't tell you how many times I've sat under that tree reading, listening to her favorite songs, just talking to her. I feel safe there. At home. With her. And that's why I get so frustrated when people mess up my name; it feels like they're disrespecting her. And I won't stand for that."

"Maggie..." He struggled to find his next words.

I cut him off. "My dad moved into a new condo recently, and it broke my heart that we had to sell the house with Gram's tree. Luckily, the family that moved in was really nice and told me I could come back whenever I wanted. Which I do pretty often."

"Wow. I never would've imagined all that was behind a name. Mine was probably just something my parents picked out off a google search."

We both laughed.

"You know, your nose scrunches when you laugh."

Was that a compliment? An insult?

"Your grandmother sounds a lot like you. She would've loved that tree."

He had moved toward me and was standing close now, too close.

Why can't I move my feet?

I looked up, meeting his bright green eyes; they'd caught just the right light from the moon. I didn't want to look away, but I knew I should.

"You know what else Gram loved?" Before he could answer my question, I yanked his arm and ran directly into the water.

"Swimming!" We were both tripping over our own feet. "We're from the Great Lakes State, remember?"

He splashed face first into the water, and I followed shortly behind. He pushed my head under the water. When I came up for air, he was shaking his head at me, all while maintaining the biggest smile I'd ever seen on his face.

"You know I'm going to get you back for this, Magnolia."

And he did get me back...*eventually*.

CHAPTER TEN

After that night at the lake, Nic seemed...lighter. His face, the way he moved, his mood, for sure. Fran even noticed one morning at breakfast. She told Nic that he seemed particularly "chipper" that day, a word I never thought would be used to describe that man. Overall, I was just happy that he was doing better. I hoped that this Nic, the real Nic, was here to stay.

He'd started spending evenings with the family after dinner. Usually we would all watch a movie. Sometimes, we played Pictionary. Once, we played Monopoly. Won't do that again.

Nic wasn't talkative, which I loved, but he was witty. He would make these hilarious comments, totally deadpan, at the perfect moment, and crack us all up. Well, most of us. August clearly didn't find him as funny as the rest of us. I really wanted to ask him what his problem with Nic was, but, frankly, I didn't want to even say Nic's name around him. August was already overly focused on him and not in a good way.

Whenever August and I managed to sneak away for a quick

moment, he would spend half the time complaining about how he'd rather have Nic go back to being distant and aloof. I let this type of comment slide the first few times, but I finally got so sick of it that I lost my temper one night out at the shed.

We were kissing, and I was trying to enjoy the only intimate moment we'd had in a while. It was about 11:00 pm. He literally stopped kissing me just so he could bitch and moan about Nic.

"I just don't get it. One day, he's all depressed and crying in his room, refusing to talk to any of us, let alone come down and watch a movie with us. Then, out of nowhere, he's like a little kid at Disney World."

His hands remained around my waist, but he was staring past my head directly into the shed, like he was searching for the answer somewhere in between the shovels and the rakes.

I rolled my eyes, frustrated that this seemed to be the only thing August cared about lately. Especially since I was right here in front of him. I doubted he even noticed that I was upset by his comments. He just kept talking like he was enjoying the sound of his own voice a little too much.

"Like, I know it's not because of a girl because we're all stuck here in quarantine. Fran hasn't even been letting him see Jack or Elliott, and I highly doubt Bel, mom, or dad are brightening his mood. So then there's you and me. I know with absolute certainty that I'm not part of the equation. So that leaves...you." He pressed his body straight up against mine.

"I know you lift my mood...among other things."

If I hadn't been so annoyed with him right then, this might've been cute. But I'd had enough. I pushed him off of me, maybe with a tad too much force. He sprung back, shocked and confused.

"August, I need you to stop obsessing over Nic. You can't even kiss me for 10 seconds without stopping to hypothesize about why he's in a good mood. Who gives a shit why? Shouldn't we just be happy for him? That he's finally figured out a way to grieve for Ellie without being a massive jerk in the process?"

He stared at me, his head cocked slightly to the right.

"He told you about Ellie?"

Was that supposed to be a secret?

"Uh, yeah," I said, trying not to seem guilty for something that I had no reason to feel guilty about. I just knew August, and this was the type of thing he would get upset about.

"That morning he was helping me out in the vineyard, you know, when we came back in and you were all eating breakfast, we just got to talking, and somehow Ellie came up. It's such a horrible story. I can't imagine how awful that must've been for him." I was looking slightly down, remembering the pain in Nic's eyes when he had let me in and told me about the accident and the last sunrise.

"So you guys went out there early in the morning to talk about your exes?"

"What? August, did you not hear me? We were out there, and I mentioned something that I guess reminded him of Ellie. He told me the story, and we came inside. That was it."

There was no way I was going to tell August that Nic and I had spent that early morning in the Lillian barn sharing a profoundly meaningful experience. That was just for me and Nic.

He shook his head, letting out a small giggle under his breath.

"Typical. He shouldn't be talking about that stuff with you; it's not your job to be his therapist. Next time, just tell him to piss off. Give him a taste of his own medicine."

How could August be so cold about this? I'm sure that he must've known Ellie too. Nic said she spent a lot of time out here on the vineyard. I definitely thought her death would have affected him at least a little. This was an ugly and bleak side to August that I wish I hadn't seen.

"I'm not going to tell him that. If he needs a friend to talk to about it, I'm willing to listen. Especially if it means he's going to be happier. We can all benefit from a happier Nic, you know." I put my arms on his shoulders, trying to convince him that my conversations and friendship with Nic were absolutely no threat to him.

He leaned in slowly and began kissing me. But this kiss was different. Much more intense, as if our conversation had lit a fire in him, like he had something to prove. He had my hips pinned against the shed, and I could feel his heart beating; his chest was pressed tightly against mine. No matter how annoyed I was, this man was fire.

Suddenly, we heard the door to the house open and close somewhat loudly. We broke apart immediately. "Who the hell was that?" I whispered.

August shook his head and shrugged.

"Did they slam the door?" I was concerned that we had been seen.

"No, I think it just closed."

"It sounded kind of loud, like a slam."

"Maggie, don't be paranoid. It was probably just Leone taking out the garbage or something."

"Okay, I'm going to go in first, and you have to wait at least five minutes before you come in. And make up a reason you were out here if anyone is in the kitchen."

He nodded and kissed my cheek.

August and I both made it upstairs without seeing anyone. We whispered good night to each other and retreated to our rooms.

Waking up the next morning, I was still concerned about last night. Who was that, and had they somehow seen us? I remembered August's unkind words about Nic. He actually wanted his own brother to be miserable. Why did he hate him? Was it all because of Nic and Lucy at that 100 days dance? August did say that he and Nic hadn't spoken about it since it happened.

I rolled over and realized Bel had already gotten up. I didn't even hear her leave the room this morning. Before getting up, I knocked on the wall quietly. Two knocks came back almost immediately; I was glad to know that August had not gone downstairs yet either.

If somehow our secret was out, we were at least going down there to face it together. I quickly threw on a pair of distressed jeans and a grey tie-dye crewneck.

I was walking to the bathroom to brush my teeth when I was swiftly grabbed into August's room. He closed the door and then kissed me softly. "Good morning, beautiful."

"Good morning," I said, kissing his cheek. "I'm going to brush my teeth, and then we'll go down together, okay?"

He nodded, already throwing on a grey t-shirt and a pair of black sweats over the boxers he had slept in.

He didn't seem too worried about his family knowing about us; sometimes, it seemed like he wanted to tell them. This made me smile because it meant he was proud of me and wanted to show me off. But I knew that was a terrible idea. We had to play it safe. If we told them and things got really awkward, I couldn't exactly board the next plane to the U.S.

I realized I was doing the staring thing again as he pulled his t-shirt over his adorable bed head. His curls were always flat right when he woke up but somehow, they still perfectly framed his flawless face. Okay, stop it! I had to stay focused.

After I brushed my teeth and combed my hair, we headed down the stairs; he trailed behind me casually.

When we arrived in the kitchen, it looked like a perfectly normal Sunday morning at the vineyard. Thank god. Maybe we didn't have anything to worry about after all.

Leone was reading the morning paper, Fran was pouring us some coffee, and Bel was watching some YouTube influencer while she scarfed down a biscuit slathered with butter and honey. Nic was eating a bowl of cereal, barely lifting his head for us when we appeared. It seemed a typical morning at the Costelli breakfast table.

"Good morning, sleepy heads, it's nearly 10! Rough night?" Fran winked at the two of us as she passed us each a mug full of piping hot coffee. I laughed while grabbing the mug from her.

Was it Fran?

Does she know?

My paranoia was going to eat me alive. I took a deep breath.

"No ma'am, just couldn't sleep with all the sleep-talking happening in our room." I smirked at Bel across the table. This was my hopefully not-too-obvious attempt to steer the conversation toward any topic other than what August and I were doing last night.

"For the millionth time, Maggie, I do not sleep-talk! I will not believe this lie until you record me or something. I think you must be hearing things." I smiled at her. "Mom, are any of the doctors' offices in town still open during quarantine? Maggie needs her ears cleaned." She threw a tiny piece of her biscuit at me.

I let out a dramatic gasp and touched my hand to my heart, my mouth open in feigned disbelief.

"Fran, trust me. My ears are perfectly clear. I know what I heard," I winked at Bel. She stuck her tongue out at me and retreated back to her phone.

Okay. Breathe, Maggie. Everything is fine. We're fine.

There was a lull.

Then: "Not sure how you could've heard Bel sleep-talking all the way from the shed." Nic spoke slowly and clearly.

Holy shit, it was Nic.

Of course it was.

Bel was immediately intrigued. She looked up, phone in hand. Leone lowered his newspaper ever-so-slightly. Fran just continued to wipe down the kitchen counter.

"The shed?" I looked at him like he was crazy. "Now we have

124

one Costelli sleep-talking and the other hallucinating," I said, trying desperately to reroute the conversation. I was full-on fake laughing now.

"I wasn't dreaming, Maggie."

I nudged August under the table, hoping he would somehow take the lead on this.

"What's he talking about? Why were you out in the shed at night, Maggie?" Bel looked genuinely confused; any hope of a smile had disappeared from her face completely.

Time to come up with something good here.

"I forgot my sweatshirt out there. I was trying to sleep, and I couldn't figure out what I was forgetting, but I knew there was something. I remembered taking it off somewhere outside when we were working so I just went out to try and look for it. Nic, you must've seen me circling the shed a hundred times. I didn't bring my phone, and it was too dark to see without a flashlight." I took a long, long sip of coffee.

Another lull.

"So that's the story you guys decided on?" He finally broke his gaze with me and shifted his focus to August. "I don't know...," he said, shaking his head. "Could've been a bit more creative than that, dude." August hadn't said a word. *Until now.*

"Watch it, Nic. You don't know what you're talking about." August was focused on Nic like a laser.

"I know exactly what I'm talking about, and soon, everyone else will too! Now, it's up to you whether I tell them or you do. Take your pick, bro."

"Maggie, what is he talking about?" Bel was looking directly at me, waiting for me to confess.

Fran had finally stopped cleaning and was standing at the counter with a look on her face that screamed: someone please explain what the hell is going on? We had the entire family's direct attention; there was absolutely no way out of this.

"Nic, I told you to watch yourself." August was standing now, towering over me. He was getting angrier by the second, not because the family was about to find out, but because Nic was threatening him.

"What are you going to do? You're all talk, but you're so full of shit." Nic spat the words back at him. He stood as he spoke.

"Why are you so fucking obsessed with me and Maggie? Live your life, and we'll live ours."

"Ours?" He cocked his head, "You two are enough of an item to refer to your lives in tandem?"

"An item? You two?" Fran didn't sound angry; however, her smile quickly faded.

"I knew it," Bel said, now standing as well. "Your stupid knocking every night. I should've trusted my gut."

"Bel, I'm so sorry. I didn't mean for it to come out like this." We were all standing now except for Leone who stayed extremely calm per usual.

She refused to look at me. This was going horribly. There was silence for about twenty seconds. Then Nic spoke.

"Does she know that you always do this? Everyone knows August, the famous tourist slayer, known for preying on young

American girls in the Florence clubs just to dump them at the end of the summer."

I literally felt like I was going to throw up. My face was hot, and my eyes filled with tears.

"ME? I'm the tourist slayer? Oh, that's a good one. What about that tourist of yours?"

Nic kicked his chair with ridiculous force; it flew across the kitchen floor and slammed into the wall. Bel gasped with pure fear. I was crying as I watched and listened in horror.

"Boys! Stop it immediately!" I had never heard Fran shout like that.

"Don't you dare talk about her like that." Nic slammed his fists down onto the table, completely ignoring Fran's plea and shaking all the bowls and mugs as if an earthquake had come through.

August had him right where he wanted him. He knew what he needed to say to provoke him. And I knew August enough to know that what was about to come out of his mouth was going to hurt like hell.

"You just had to have her come out one last time to see your perfect little set-up. Like she gave a shit. You think you were the only one she was doing? She just felt sorry for you. And look what it cost her."

That was the final straw.

In a flash, Nic had grabbed the side of the table with both hands and pushed the whole thing about six feet to the side. He lunged at August, throwing an off-kilter punch that sent him flying back. He crashed into the pots and pans hanging on the wall.

Fran looked horrified. She was holding Bel and yelling at them to stop.

August pushed Nic straight through the screen door, and they were now throwing each other around in the grass. It was absolutely pouring rain. Fran continued to hold Bel, trying to shield her from seeing her brothers acting like two heathens who want to rip each other's faces off.

Leone ran out the door and stood over them.

"ENOUGH!"

The boys were so shocked by the rage that had escaped from their typically calm and collected father that they both just stopped and stared at him. His voice seemed to echo for miles.

He looked down at them. "You are humiliating yourselves. Quit acting like fools, and start acting like the men your mother and I raised you to be."

They both released their grips. August slowly stood up and offered his hand down to Nic to help him up, an amicable gesture I wouldn't have expected out of him.

Nic swatted his hand away and got up on his own, only to take off in a sprint up the gravel road. He was out of sight within minutes.

Leone looked at August with disgust, then turned and went inside without a word. August followed slowly behind him, soaking wet and filthy, his head hung low. When he entered through the side door, Fran, not looking at him, held out a towel.

"We're going to discuss this later. Get upstairs now; you've done enough damage today." August acknowledged her request silently and headed for the staircase. When he passed me, I mouthed, "I'm sorry."

"Maggie, take the car, and go find Nic." Fran ordered me without offering me a chance to say no. "He runs fast so he could be pretty far by now. Please. Go now."

Fran sounded scared. She wouldn't look at me.

As I headed toward the door, Leone took Fran into his arms, and she started crying.

"Sono spaventato."

Leone responded, "Stara bene."

I took the keys to the Jeep off the hook next to the door and exited the kitchen without saying a word.

I drove down the gravel and could feel the tires sliding as the rain crashed against the windshield. I turned on the bright headlights so I could hopefully see Nic running along the side of the road.

He was fast. I had been driving for 5 minutes, and there was still no sign of him.

I started to panic. What if I couldn't find him and he did something...Nic was still grieving regardless of the good days he'd had recently. There was really no telling what he could do. I turned around and tried to retrace my steps. Maybe I missed him.

I sped up. I was going much faster than I should've been on an unpaved, nearly flooded road. The windshield wipers moved back and forth at the fastest speed possible, but I could still barely see anything. I squinted, desperately trying to make out anything resembling a large, angry human.

The steering wheel started to shake. Then everything started to shake. Before I could even think to pull the emergency brake, I was tasting a mouthful of airbag. I had gone off the road and hit a large tree head on and dented the entire front hood of the Jeep.

Jesus, why me? *Why?!*

I was extremely disoriented; I was trying to push the airbag back into the wheel for some reason. Smoke was spewing out from the hood, and the rain continued to pour down.

I glanced up at my reflection in the rear view mirror and, thankfully, only had a small red mark above my right eye where the airbag had made contact. No blood, but my head was throbbing, I felt nauseated, and I just really needed to rest my head for a minute. I laid my head back on the seat and felt myself drifting off.

I don't know how long I was laying there asleep, but when I woke up, I was being lifted out of the car by a tall, familiar, soaking wet figure. I blinked a few times trying to make out who was carrying me and fighting back the dizziness and confusion.

"Holy shit. Maggie, it's okay. You're okay." The voice was familiar.

"August?" I called out with my eyes shut.

There was a pause. Everything was blurry, including sounds. I kept blinking, hoping the clarity would magically return.

"It's Nic, Mags. I'm here."

I felt a wave of comfort flood over me as I relaxed in his arms.

Still carrying me, he managed to open the back of the jeep and pick up the blanket that Fran kept there for occasions such as this, shut the back door, and spread the blanket on the ground.

He gently placed me in a seated position on the blanket and sat down next to me. My eyes were so heavy. He brushed the hair back from my face.

"Mags, come on. You gotta keep your eyes open. Look at me."

His voice was shaking, and it almost sounded like he might be crying. Everything was still too fuzzy for me to be sure. It wasn't until he leaned over and kissed my forehead that I remembered.

Ellie.

It had taken Nic so long to forgive himself for Ellie's accident. And now, here I was, sprawled on the ground after yet another one.

I looked at him briefly before wrapping my arms around his neck. He seemed shocked by this but quickly returned the gesture.

"Ow." I winced.

"Oh god, I'm sorry. Does it hurt? Where? Maggie, what the hell? You scared the shit out of me."

He was squeezing me even tighter than a few seconds ago, and it hurt my rib cage like hell, but I let him.

"Nic, I'm fine. I'm okay. Everything's okay."

He pulled away and looked me directly in the eye.

"This is all my fault. I shouldn't have run. I didn't think you'd come after me. I just needed to get away and think and...get really really wet." We both laughed.

"I promise I'm okay." He seemed to finally accept this; he nodded slowly.

"I'm so sorry, Mags. I would never have been able to forgive myself if…you…god, why do I keep hurting people I love."

Love.

It slipped out. Right?

I closed my eyes again and rested my head against his chest, focusing on taking deep breaths. We stayed like this for a few minutes.

I couldn't help replaying in my brain what Nic had said.

People I love.

I know that trauma and fear make people say things they don't necessarily mean. And it makes sense that he loves me. As a friend. As a sister.

And I love him like that, too.

But this, this moment. All of it feels...I don't know...different?

He helped me stand. He then picked me up again in his arms. I didn't even try to protest. I was still so dizzy that I don't think I could have made it back to the house alone even if I'd tried.

Neither of us had our phones — I hadn't even taken my purse, which was pretty stupid. So we would have to tell Fran about the Jeep when we got back. Surprisingly, I wasn't nervous about telling her I wrecked the car. I was, however, nervous about showing up at the house in Nic's arms. August would surely have a field day with that one.

Nic carried me the entire time. Thankfully, the rain had let up. He didn't seem to get tired at all carrying me over a mile back to the house. I tried to keep my eyes open, but his arms were so comforting that I felt myself dozing off a few times, resting against his chest. Before we stepped into the house, Nic paused and looked down at me.

"I'm so glad you're okay. But don't do anything stupid like that again. Don't come after me next time. I don't need rescuing, especially if it means you get hurt in the process." He spoke softly and calmly, but his words still sent a weird feeling through my stomach.

What did he mean, "next time?"

God, I really hoped there wouldn't be a next time that I have to run after my boyfriend's brother who just got done punching my boyfriend in the face. When I thought about it like that, this whole situation sounded really fucked up.

"Okay, I won't."

"Good."

He managed to open the side door, still holding me tightly.

What was he, a ninja?

Fran and Bel were sitting at the table. Fran jumped out of her chair and rushed toward us.

"What the hell happened, Nic? Maggie? Are you okay?"

Nic very slowly put me down and led me to a chair.

"Someone better tell me what happened, now. Bel, go get Maggie some ice for her head."

"Fran, I'm so sorry. I was driving in circles looking for Nic. The road was flooded. I couldn't see anything. Somehow I went off the road and hit a tree."

"Mom, it's not her fault. I shouldn't have run away like that, I just needed to clear my head. I didn't think anyone would come after me."

"Oh Maggie, I'm sorry." Fran surveyed the freshly forming bruise surrounding my eye. "I should've known with all that rain that it wouldn't be safe. I...wasn't thinking clearly. I'm so sorry. Are you okay?"

"Yeah, I'm fine! Growing up with brothers left me with worse, trust me."

She let out a tiny smile lined with relief. "Where's the car?"

"It's about a mile down the road. I'm not sure it's drive-able. I just wanted to get her back here, but I can go back out and check if you want."

"No, not right now. It should be okay there for a bit, and then I'll go with you."

"Fran, I'll pay for the repairs. This is my fault. I was driving. I'm so so sorry." I felt like a broken record with the amount of times I'd apologized to this poor woman.

She shook her head.

"Mom, she's been falling asleep since the crash. I think she might have a concussion." Nic looked at me when he spoke, but I remained fixated on the table in front of me.

Bel handed me a bag of ice with a dish towel wrapped around it.

"Nic, I'm fine. Seriously, guys. I just need some ice and a little nap, and I'll be good as new."

Suddenly, everyone (except me) was on his or her phone, looking up information on concussions.

"Okay, this says the concussive person may be confused, irritable, or sad. If she can carry on a conversation and is walking alright, then she's okay to sleep." Bel looked at me dead-on and crossed her arms. "Can you walk, Maggie?"

"Yeah...I can walk. Do you want to see?

"Yeah, I want to see." Bel's face was just so done.

"No problem."

I pushed myself up and out of my chair. Nic slid over to me, no doubt to catch me if I fell. I began walking toward the stairs, Nic following behind. It was about eight steps. Easy-peasy. I turned and walked the eight steps back like a model on a runway. I was determined, for some reason, to show her I could walk successfully.

I sat back down, looking at Bel triumphantly. She rolled her eyes.

"Nic, could you go get me my hoody off my bed?"

"Bel, there's like a million hoodies in the mud room."

"Just go get it, okay?"

Nic got the point and left the room, shaking his head. He trudged up the stairs slowly, sneaking glances at us as he went.

It was now just me, Fran, and Bel in the kitchen. A very painful moment of silence occurred before I decided to begin my official apology tour.

"Fran, Bel, I'm so sorry. If I would've known how much trouble this would cause, how much chaos this would stir up, I never would've even considered..."

"But you did know." Bel cut me off. "I told you. I tried to warn you that something like this, chaos, that is, would happen. They're both extreme hot heads. You just saw how mean August can be, and Nic...I know he's been doing well, but since Ellie, part of him is just...broken. Is this what you want?"

Fran held up her hand. "Stop. Don't talk about your brothers like that."

"No, keep going, please." Nic was standing in the doorway to the kitchen, hoody in hand.

Bel exhaled and looked down. "I was just trying to protect you."

"Protect me? From what?"

Bel was silent.

"Why are you even involved in this, Bel? This has nothing to do with you."

Bel stood up and headed toward the stairs, muttering, "Fucking selfish and pathetic," she muttered under her breath, still loud enough for all of us to hear.

"Right." Nic let out a sarcastic chuckle.

Just before Bel disappeared from sight, she turned sharply. "At least he can admit he likes her and actually do something about it. News flash, idiot. She's made her choice."

"Fuck you Bel."

"Nicolo Costelli, don't you dare speak to your sister like that. Both of you, upstairs now." Fran snapped, clearly having heard enough.

I felt so uncomfortable; I couldn't even bear to look up at any of them.

Bel ran. Nic lingered for a moment, looking down at his shoes.

"Nic, go upstairs." Fran was firm with her instruction. Nic stood still for a few seconds before turning and making his way heavily up the stairs.

I wanted to say so much to Fran right now, apologize a hundred more times, but nothing came out.

I know I said that I'd always wanted to know what having a disappointed parent felt like, what having a parent who cared enough to notice your mistakes felt like, but I completely regretted that wish now that I had disappointed Fran.

She suddenly stood up. I knew now that we were alone, she was about to scold me, and rightfully so. To my surprise, she made her way around the table, gave my shoulder one slow, firm pat, gripping it for just a moment, before retreating to her bedroom silently.

This was both comforting and terrifying.

CHAPTER ELEVEN

I sat at the table alone for a few minutes trying to process what had just happened. This was basically my attempt to put off going upstairs and confronting Bel. I knew I would be walking directly into her continued wrath.

And I definitely couldn't stand the thought of talking to Nic right now.

The entire house was eerily quiet. I closed my eyes and took a deep breath, embracing the rarity of the stillness.

When I opened my eyes, I gasped.

Leone was standing on the other side of the table, completely silent. I didn't even hear him walk into the kitchen.

He and I hadn't talked much; he was genuinely so calm and quiet, always observing everything. I respect people who don't have to try to command every room they walk into with constant talking.

"Oh my gosh, Leone. I'm so sorry...I didn't see you standing there."

He pulled a chair out and sat down across from me. I was

attempting to read the expression on his face as he folded his hands together on the table.

"Maggie," he started. "I hope you're not beating yourself up for this too much. What happened today was not your fault."

This was not at all what I had been expecting to come out of his mouth. His voice was tender and soft; he reminded me of my dad.

"Now that the storm is, hopefully, over, you're left with a tough decision. Those of us with hearts too big for our own good, we're ready to love anything and everything in our path. We have hearts that never sleep."

He was such an eloquent speaker when he actually spoke. His words were truly poetic. And the fact that he'd said, "those of us with hearts too big" made me wonder if we had more in common than I would've thought.

"I'm sorry, Leone. All of this could've been avoided tonight if I'd just…"

"Love can't be avoided, Maggie. Especially love like the love I witnessed rolling around on the lawn earlier. You can move continents away, you can try to bury it, drown it, swallow it whole, love persists. Believe that." He stood up slowly.

I wasn't sure what to say in response to this so I just sat and observed his careful movements. He walked slowly away from the table and paused right before he entered the doorway to his and Fran's bedroom. His hesitation led me to believe there was more he wanted to say but couldn't find the words.

"Hey, Leone?" He turned to face me now.

"Thank you. You and Fran have both been so generous and kind to me. I promise you won't have to deal with any more drama."

He smiled gently as his eyes traveled from the ground back up to me.

"Knowing those two sons of mine, I highly doubt that."

This time there was no hesitation in his step. He turned quickly and entered the bedroom, closing the door gingerly behind him.

I was left alone again in the stillness; the silence filled the room and wrapped me up. It was so strange for there to be utter silence in this house in the middle of the day. I was paralyzed by the conversation I'd just had with Leone.

I hadn't told anyone that I had even the slightest interest in being more than friends with Nic. But Leone knew that there was something special there. He had probably known this whole time, maybe before I did. That's the thing about the quiet ones: they are constantly listening and soaking up all of life's tiny and seemingly insignificant details.

The longer I sat and processed Leone's words, particularly the part where he blatantly said, "you're left with a tough decision," the more anxious I started to feel. What did he mean? There was no decision. I was with August. And we had a good relationship even though it was still pretty new. We were at that point where you start to realize that the other person is not perfect and that there are some imperfections that you just have to learn to live with. Like August's temper.

Nic and I are friends. There may be a few sparks here and there, but we are in close quarters and he's very attractive so that's bound to happen. Right?

If I were Bec, I would have already put together a detailed pros and cons list for each of them.

My relationship with August was probably the most electrifying thing to ever happen to me. I'd never before felt the rush I got when he stared at me like he wanted to devour me and didn't even try to hide it. He had very clearly shown his interest in me from the second we met, and I hadn't had to work for his attention or affection at all. He just gave it freely. Our chemistry was off the charts. Most of the time, he was so sweet and funny. I could go on and on about all of August's amazing qualities.

But he could also be intense and aggressive, and his temper was worrisome. I was sickened by what he had said to Nic about Ellie. It was just cruel. And Nic didn't deserve that.

Nic had completely changed in the past month or so. I'd witnessed such growth in him. He didn't need anyone to save him. He was saving himself and learning to live with his grief. I think what he always needed was a real friend. Someone who didn't pass off his behavior as "Nic just being Nic" or, like Bel, seeing him as broken.

The real Nic was kind, compassionate, hilarious, and so sweet. He had a sensitivity about him and a gentleness that most guys, including August, didn't possess. He wasn't afraid to be vulnerable. He was definitely passionate, and he obviously could be provoked to the point of acting out physically. But could I really blame him for punching August after what he'd said?

This was too much thinking for me. I was exhausted, physically and emotionally, and I just needed to shut my brain off.

I took a deep breath and slowly stood up. I made my way to the stairs, preparing to explain myself to Bel. With each step, I used the railing to pull myself up. Pain shot through my head and my left side simultaneously. When was that pain med going to kick in?

I knocked quietly while pushing the door to our room open to find Bel laying on her bed with headphones on. This girl watched more YouTube than anyone I'd ever met, but I guess she needed a distraction. I didn't blame her. A distraction sounded really good about now.

When she saw me, she maintained the same disappointed look from downstairs.

Am I really about to be disciplined by a 16-year-old?

Bel cracked her knuckles like she was preparing to beat me up. She was taking a much more combative approach than Leone had, but I could handle it. I would just nod and agree with her because no matter how much I didn't want to admit it, she was normally right.

"Maggie, I literally told you to stay away from them. And you did the exact opposite. I could've told you something like this would happen."

I looked down at my lap.

"I've never seen them like this. No girl has ever come between them like you have, Maggie."

Damn it.

Does August know for certain that Nic has feelings for me? When I don't even know that?

I'm so confused.

"Bel, I'm not sure Nic likes me in the way you think he does. He needed a friend. I was there for him."

She laughed mockingly.

"You're blind if you can't see that Nic is jealous. Why do you think he's been hanging out with the family so much? It's so he can hang out with you, Maggie. He didn't just get better. He got better because he fell in love with you. It's pretty obvious. And he knows it's real. He's terrified to be in another relationship. That's why he's had nothing but one-night stands in the past year. And he should be terrified because he's not ready. He may look fine on the outside now, but the inside is still really messed up. A relationship right now would be disastrous for him. I just know it.

Did I just hear Bel say that Nic is…in love with me?

"You should've just told me about August. I could've helped you, protected you, even. I thought you trusted me. I know he's my brother, but I thought we were friends."

She wasn't mad anymore, just hurt that I hadn't shared this with her.

"I'm sorry, Bel. So sorry."

"Maggie, they both clearly have feelings for you. You need to accept that. It's your feelings you need to sort out now. You can't have them both. You have to choose if you want to stop hurting them. Or if you want them to stop hurting each other. You have to choose."

Why did everyone keep telling me I had to choose!?

I DON'T WANT TO CHOOSE.

I REFUSE. I CHOOSE NOT TO CHOOSE.

Okay. Let's think about this rationally. The reality was that I was already in a relationship with August and, even if I wanted to, I couldn't exactly break up with him and start seeing his brother while we're all living together. I would obviously have to leave in that scenario. And I should listen to Bel about Nic not being ready to be in another relationship. I could never forgive myself if I was responsible for him relapsing. But the main point is that I may already be in love with August or headed that way. And Nic and I are friends. And I don't want that to change. I want everything to stay the way it is.

Bel turned over in her bed and put the headphones back on. It didn't feel like our conversation was over, but I took that as a sign to let it go for now.

I had to make this right.

First, I needed to talk to August.

I knocked on the wall, hoping, praying for an answer.

August knocked back, twice, which prompted me to immediately jump out of bed and move as swiftly as I could to his room. Bel knew where I was going, but she let me go without any critique. August was lying on his bed holding a bag of frozen carrots on his left eye, which was terribly bruised and swollen from Nic's fist.

"Where have you been?"

"Uh, I was in a bit of an accident." I sat down on the bed next to him.

He sat up in a flash and threw the bag of carrots on the bed. He examined my face, which I doubt looked anywhere near cute.

"A car accident? What do you mean? Why were you driving?"

144

"After the fight, Fran asked me to go find Nic. She really didn't give me a choice, August. She practically pushed me out the door. I didn't want to upset her any further so I just went."

There was a flash of anger in his eyes. He really really didn't like hearing that I went after Nic instead of coming up to be with him after the fight, but he let me continue.

"I couldn't find him, and it got dark, and I got frustrated, and the road was basically flooded. I went off the road and hit a tree. The airbags were released and I'm okay. I think I got a minor concussion, but I'm okay." August's face hung low. He was staring at the floor. After I finished telling him about the accident, he slowly nodded. He was clearly still hung up on the fact that I'd gone after Nic.

"August, I'm sorry. We should have just told everyone straight up about us."

He gingerly swung his legs around so that we were sitting side by side on the bed. I could tell he was trying not to wince so he could look strong and impress me. He reached out and placed his hand on top of my thigh, giving it a gentle yet firm squeeze.

"Maggie, it's okay. This isn't your fault. Nic and I were going to have to deal with our issues at some point. I guess this was just an opportunity for us to speak our truths, or punch our truths." He let out a tiny laugh.

"I know, but if I hadn't have ever come here, you guys wouldn't be fighting over me."

I realized literally as the words were coming out of my mouth, that I had made a mistake. A big fucking mistake. Could I blame it on the concussion?

There was a very unpleasant pause.

"What do you mean, fighting over you?" he said in response to my comment. "What's there to fight over?" He sounded genuinely confused.

I can save this. Somehow, I can save this.

"No, I didn't mean, like, fighting OVER me, or like FOR me or anything...I just meant if I had never come to the vineyard, this argument probably wouldn't have happened." He wasn't buying it. He sat up taller, disregarding the pain.

He was looking intently into my eyes, and I could tell his brain was going a mile a minute. He was trying to decide if I was lying or not.

Why was my heart pounding? I had nothing to hide.

Did I?

I couldn't speak. I had no idea what to say.

"Is that why he was so upset when he saw us out by the shed?" He had that fake-amused look on his face.

I was concentrating on trying not to look guilty, but he was smarter, quicker than me.

"Oh...my...god." August stood up. "I knew that he wouldn't have been that mad about us simply not telling the family. Now it makes sense. Wow. It's pathetic, Maggie. He's fucking pathetic." He laughed sarcastically. He was pacing now.

"God, I'm such an idiot! I should've seen it. Of course he likes you. That's why he's been better. And here I was, thinking I was getting my brother back, that he was finally getting over the Ellie thing and snapping out of his never-ending depressive episode. But it was never about him wanting to spend time with me or the family. He was just trying to get close to you so he could get in your pants. So fucking typical of him. Always jealous of my life."

Hearing August bash Nic pissed me off.

Because, once again, Nic did not deserve it.

"August, stop! What is it with you? Your brother went through something absolutely horrible. And you talk about it like it's nothing. You knew Ellie, right? She fucking died. Your brother loved her. God...what you said earlier...I don't know that August...and I don't want to know him. And Nic's not trying to get in my pants. He and I are friends. Good friends."

"Are you kidding me right now?! Stop protecting him! Since when do you defend him over me? I thought we were together, but apparently, you've been up to something else, or should I say someone else."

"I'm the one who's been up to something else? What about all that "tourist slayer" shit Nic was talking about?" I dramatically enacted the air quotes. "Sounds like you've been pretty busy too, hot shot."

His eyes widened quickly before sinking back to the floor. Like he had just been caught. The way we were talking to each other was so childish, but I wasn't going to let him push me around.

"Jesus, Maggie. He was just trying to upset me."

August was a bad liar.

"Well... it upset me instead, so could you please explain it for me?"

I could see his chest rise and fall as he took a large, deep breath.

What was he about to tell me?

August's words were measured. "Nic was exaggerating, as usual. He was just talking about how I used to date a lot of tourists."

"Really? Like, how many?" I had a sick feeling in my gut.

"Maggie, all that shit is in the past. None of it matters."

I didn't move a muscle and maintained my steely gaze on him.

After about 20 seconds of us staring at each other silently, I could tell that he had decided to tell me some version of the truth. He'd probably realized that Nic would just tell me if he didn't.

"I need you to promise not to get mad, okay? It's just stupid shit from a million years ago."

"Just tell me." I had no intention of "not getting mad."

When will men learn to stop telling women not to get mad at things? Insider secret... it just makes us more mad.

"Okay...so...in high school, during the summers, my friends and I had this kind of...competition... where we would see how many tourists we could...you know..."

My head cocked quickly to the right and I felt my stomach drop. It wasn't the fact that he had been with multiple other girls before me. I could handle that. Hell, I'd assumed that. It was more the fact that he and his friends had made a game out of it. That was sick. He reached for my hands, and I pulled them away.

"Maggie, I know it sounds bad, but it was just stupid high school shit. And, if it makes you feel any better, I didn't even win! I came in third place!"

"August, shut up! I don't want to hear about it! Any of it! It's disgusting."

I stood up, biting my lip, trying to hold back the countless other insults I wanted to hurl at him. Neither of us said anything for the next two minutes.

A horrible thought came into my head.

"So, was that what I was? The night we met at Silk? Was I part of your little game? Another tally mark on your tourist to-do list?"

He charged at me and pressed my body tightly against the wall.

"Maggie, look at me."

I refused, until he lifted my chin to meet his gaze.

"Maggie, you've got it so incredibly wrong. Meeting you that night at Silk was the most unexpected and amazing gift for me. I was so taken with you, I forgot to ask for your number, or even your last name, for god's sake. You were never part of some stupid game or joke. And when...when I saw you here that first night, when I came out of the shower, I couldn't believe it. I thought I was never going to see you again. And there you were. So fucking beautiful and radiant and right here in my house! I promise, you're not just some girl. You're THE girl. MY girl. I'll never let you go."

It was kind of shameful how I already wanted to forgive him. If I could forgive him, life would be easier. He did have a way with words. And we all had a past. I sure as hell did.

"And...with Nic...you're right. It was awful when Ellie died. It doesn't matter what I thought of her. What I said was disrespectful. It wasn't his fault. I'm really sorry, babe."

He began kissing me slowly, teasing me, not giving me a chance to respond. And I was so incredibly relieved to hear him saying what he was saying, that I let him. It was definitely not a resolution to our argument, but it was an okay start.

My head still hurt from the accident, and I wasn't exactly sure how we were going to move forward from all this, but, at this moment, I didn't care. I gave in to the warmth of his soft lips and his strong hands moving up and down my back. His hands slid down my ass, and he lifted me up. I wrapped my legs around his waist and felt him press harder against me. He suddenly pulled his head back; there was only a centimeter between our lips now.

He whispered, "Maggie...I think I'm in love with you."

It was at that moment, and just before he hugged me,, that Nic appeared in the hallway outside August's room.

August was facing away from the door and didn't see him, thank god. My eyes met Nic's briefly before he disappeared down the hall and into his room. I squeezed August tighter and closed my eyes.

CHAPTER TWELVE

A week had gone by, and, in that time, I had barely seen Nic at all except at dinner each night. He was obviously making a great effort to avoid August and I completely, both when we were together as well as when we were apart. I didn't blame him.

Fran had forced me to take a whole week off work with little to no screen time to make sure my concussion healed properly. She really had the whole mom thing down.

August and I tried to be courteous when it came to displays of affection around the family, although everyone had pretty much adjusted to us being an item...well, everyone except Nic, of course.

Fran even told me that she was happy we were together, which caught me by surprise. She had strict ground rules: no closed doors, no funny business. I was more than happy to abide by any rules she put in place, as long as it meant August and I could be together.

I had been living with the Costelli's for almost 3 months now. The number of COVID-19 cases had luckily been on the decline. We were still socially distancing and wearing masks any time we had to leave the house.

I had only talked to my parents a few times since arriving. They eventually wanted to speak to Fran and Leone, I guess to make sure I wasn't imposing and that they weren't serial killers, but after they got some basic info, they just let me do my thing.

I had weekly video calls with Bec and Jen. The calls normally had to be late at night when everyone else was asleep due to the time difference.

Bec always had a million questions, of course. She was mainly concerned about logistical details like how I was going to get back to the U.S., what I would do if I got the virus, and other stuff that Bec, being a Type A worrywart, simply couldn't let go of.

Jen was more interested in the love aspect, every week asking me how August was and if we were planning on having little Italian-American babies yet. I had told them about Nic and Bel too, but decided not to mention the fight for now. Being here on the vineyard felt special and separate from all other parts of my life, and there were just some things that I wanted to keep here with me. I knew someday they would pry every tiny detail out of me, probably with the help of some liquor, but for now, this place was mine. August was mine, the vineyard, all of it, just mine.

I did miss my friends and my dad, but that's about all I missed from back home. I was so busy during the day working in the vineyard and cleaning up the barns for when the wedding season came back to life that I hardly had any time to think about life back in the US.

August and I had only talked once or twice about what would

happen when I had to go back. The topic really upset him. Any time I tried to bring it up, he would just shush me and change the subject.

Things felt more and more serious each day with him ever since he told me he loved me. Our relationship was now in full throttle. I didn't say it back that night, mainly because I was shook up from Nic witnessing that intimate moment, but it didn't take long for me to find the words, and we were now one of those nauseating couples who said "I love you" every other sentence.

I took August to the lake that Nic had shown me. I didn't tell him that I had been there with Nic, of course, but said that I was bored one day and started to wander when I had stumbled upon it.

August knew about the lake and didn't really seem as mesmerized by it as I was, which disappointed me a little, but I just had to remind myself that not everyone felt a special connection to lakes, and not everyone's childhood practically revolved around them.

I tried to help him see what I saw by sharing stories of our summer house on Lake Michigan. How the fourth of July was the biggest holiday of the year, and we'd watch the fireworks from the end of the dock, and someone inevitably got pushed in. I had two older brothers, after all.

He told me he loved my stories, and he always seemed to be listening, but sometimes I felt like I was talking to myself and reliving the moments on my own rather than sharing them with someone I loved. Maybe it was uncomfortable for him to hear about my life in the U.S. because it reminded him that I had to go home at some point.

One day, after he was done with school and I was done with work, he surprised me out by the lake with a sunset picnic. It was incredibly romantic and unexpected. He was always doing small sweet gestures for me, but this was the first time he'd set something up that he knew would be really special for me.

We shared a bottle of red wine and snacked on some random things he'd grabbed from the kitchen.

As the sun went down, we lay on the blanket he'd set out for us, and I rested my head on his chest, which rose and fell with each deep slow breath he took. We didn't say much, but I knew we were both thinking, "How can anything ever be better than this moment right now?"

We were both so relaxed that we fell asleep like this before being awakened to the sound of a man's voice calling my name.

I rubbed my eyes, wondering if I was imagining the voice, until Nic emerged from the woods and stood at the edge of the sand, only a few feet from where we were lying.

"You guys are gonna want to see this."

August and I looked at each other, confused but intrigued. We didn't ask any questions; we grabbed the picnic supplies and followed him through the woods, back up the path, and into the yard.

We found Bel, Fran, and Leone all sitting at the kitchen table huddled around a laptop. Fran turned around and looked at us with a huge smile. "It's over, guys. Quarantine is over!"

Nic stood up on a chair and shouted, "WE'RE FREE!!!" Bel was running circles around the kitchen table and dancing hilariously.

I was happy for them that their business would be up and running again soon. I flashed back to when I'd first met Fran at the airport. It felt like a lifetime ago that we were sitting there on that bench, total strangers, completely unaware of the way our lives were about to change.

Honestly, I had pretty much forgotten that we were even still quarantined. I had never once felt trapped or stuck here.

I knew it was selfish of me to be sad that their country was finally healing and that people would be able to go out again, but, in that moment, I felt nothing but grief. I was the only one not wildly celebrating. Bel looked at me across the kitchen.

"Wait. Maggie, does this mean you have to leave?"

The celebration came to a sudden halt. Everyone was looking at me, anticipating my answer. I offered her a shy smile.

"I think so, Bel. I've been here for a while now. I don't want to overstay my welcome. You've all been so incredibly gracious to me; it's probably time I head back."

I always knew this was going to be a temporary arrangement. Hell, I didn't think I was going to stay here longer than that first weekend. She and Leone looked at each other briefly, and then Fran walked over and put her arm around Bel.

"You know, Maggie does have her own life back in America. I doubt she wants to stay here with us forever."

I was starting to tear up.

"Although if she did..." Fran looked over at me and raised her eyebrows. My heart began to race. "...we might be able to make this a longer arrangement."

Bel started jumping up and down.

August interjected. "What are you talking about, mom?"

Nic was silent. I met his eyes and quickly looked away.

"Well, Leone and I have been talking, and we're going to need some serious help around here now that quarantine is lifted and business is hopefully about to take off again. We'll need to travel to the US to meet with our investor pretty often this summer, and those barns aren't going to get themselves ready for the wedding season. So we were thinking…"

Fran looked at me now.

"We'd really like you to stay through the summer, Maggie. We can pay you hourly, or you can use it for internship credit at school. Whatever you need from us. We want to help you in any way we can because you staying would be more help to us than you can imagine."

I had never experienced such kindness. Before I could scream, "Yes!" Fran approached me and put her hands on my shoulders, looking at me more like a mother than my mother had in my entire life.

"You're family now, Maggie. It wouldn't be the same if you left."

I hugged her, letting out a few tears as she stroked my hair.

"Thank you, Fran. I would be so happy to stay. Seriously, thank you."

Bel was running around the kitchen again. She ran over and hugged me. August and Leone followed.

I had never seen Leone express so much affection. I squeezed him tightly.

Nic was last to hug me, whispering in my ear for only me to hear.

"I'm glad you're staying, Magnolia."

"Me too," I whispered back.

Our hug was brief, but I knew he meant what he'd said.

CHAPTER THIRTEEN

Fran wasn't joking when she'd said the summer was going to be a lot of work. If I wasn't sweating my butt off out in the barns, I was running errands in town.

I had been practicing the tour route of the vineyard, and Fran finally let me give a tour to an engaged couple who showed up one day. Luckily, they spoke English. I had always been interested in a career in wedding planning so this opportunity to work alongside Fran and Leone was perfect.

Fran also started letting me work in the office for part of the week. I was able to sit in on her calls and watch how the vineyard was run from behind the scenes, which made me love it even more. It also helped me learn more Italian.

We were nearing the end of summer, and I couldn't believe how fast it had gone. August and I had remained steady all summer; once we were out of quarantine, he showed me all his favorite spots around town and introduced me to his friends.

I was definitely worried that August and I wouldn't be able to make the distance work when I went back to Michigan and he went back to London. But what really terrified me was the thought that my life would never be as great as it was here in Italy. That this was the high point, and everything from this point forward would just pale in comparison.

The end of quarantine had turned Bel into my own personal tour guide. She was determined to show me all the best shopping spots near the vineyard. One place she'd taken me about mid-summer was a small town about 30 minutes away. We left bright and early.

We listened to American music the whole time. Bel was obsessed with The Jonas Brothers so their new album was playing on repeat. We sang along loudly with the windows down.

We pulled into the adorable little tuscan town of Montaione and parked on a side street. We walked up and down the beautiful cobblestone streets, weaving in and out of the stores.

After an hour or so of strolling around, we decided to stop for a quick bite. I heard someone approach the table.

"Bel? Sei tu?"

A beautiful blonde girl pushed her tragically expensive sunglasses up into her hair to get a better look at Bel sitting beside me.

"Lu!" Bel jumped up. "Ciao" They were hugging each other now.

"Che piacere rivederti!" The girl pulled away from the hug and brushed Bel's hair behind her ear. "I tuoi capelli sono fantastici."

Neither of them seemed to remember that I was sitting right there, but I decided to stay quiet and let them catch up.

"Mi ha ucciso non poter fare acquisti durante la quarantena."

They both let out a laugh before Bel and I made eye contact.

"Oh shit, so sorry. Lu, this is Maggie! She's been staying with us for the past few months."

I quickly stood up and reached my hand out to shake hers.

"She's American, clearly." They both laughed again as I slowly pulled my hand back.

The girl looked me up and down and not subtly before offering the slightest hint of a smile.

"Nice to meet you, Maggie. The Costelli brothers must be having a hell of a time with you."

She clearly knew their family well and wanted to make sure I knew that. I felt a surge of jealousy rush through me but decided not to play her little game.

"It's nice to meet you too!" My response was equal parts fake-nice and sarcastic.

"Well I'll let you two get back to your lunch. Bel, ci raggiungeremo presto." She hugged Bel again.

"Scrivermi."

She smiled and started to walk away before looking casually over her shoulder.

"Oh and...give the boys my love." She winked at me and slid her sunglasses back onto her beautifully tanned and flawless face. She strutted away with a sway in her tiny hips, clearly satisfied with her attempts to confuse me.

I watched her until she was out of sight. She was the type of girl who commanded your attention even if you didn't want to give it to her.

I looked over at Bel as she took a gigantic bite of our Margherita pizza. With a mouth full of food, she met my stare with a puzzled look.

"What?"

"You know what!" I snapped back sassily at her.

She swallowed her food and turned to face me. "Oh, you want to know who that girl was. Got it. Sorry."

I rolled my eyes.

"That's Lucy, but we all call her Lu."

Lucy. Wait. Why did that name seem familiar?

"She's been a family friend forever. They used to live down the road from the vineyard; that's how we all met her. But they moved a couple years ago so I haven't seen her since then. She also may have had a little…uh…thing I guess you could call it?"

"With who?"

"With Nic. Then with August."

Slut.

The way Lucy had talked about "the boys," combined with Bel's little insight, pissed me off to no end. I was trying to ignore all the unpleasant scenarios my brain was making up. And suddenly I remembered: prom.

"Maggie, I see that jealous look in your eye. Don't worry about her. She's out of the picture now."

I had a million questions. Like:

How did it end with Nic and her and August and her?

I know she doesn't talk to August but does she talk to Nic?

Does he want to talk to her?

Why the fuck does she look like that?

I took a long sip of my sangria. My head was swimming. I could tell Bel didn't want to talk about it anymore by the way she picked up her phone and completely forgot I was sitting next to her. Does she not want to talk about it because there's stuff she doesn't want me to know? I didn't fight her on it. I just sat back in my chair and tried to forget Lucy altogether; however, I feared this wouldn't be the last I'd see of her.

We sat peacefully enjoying our lunch as we people-watched.

"Hey Maggie, can I talk to you about something?" Bel's tone was more serious than I'd ever heard.

"Of course." I shifted in my seat to give her my full attention.

She took a deep breath in preparation. "I kinda...have a boyfriend."

My jaw dropped, physically and mentally. "A boyfriend?! And you're just now telling me this?! Who? How did this happen?"

"Breathe." She laughed at my frantic questioning. I couldn't help it. Bel was still a kid in my eyes, but I guess it didn't surprise me that she already had a boyfriend. She was gorgeous, after all.

"I need all the details. Let's go!"

"I know, I know. His name is Gianni, but everyone just calls him G. Um, let's see...he's a photographer. Loves dogs. Beer. You know, typical guy stuff."

"Yeah, that's not enough for me. Where did you meet? How old is he? How did I not know anything about this?"

"Just promise not to freak out, okay?"

I am not good at not freaking out, but I vowed to try my best as I nodded supportively.

"You know my friend Siena? I think I've talked about her a few times before."

"Yeah, I remember. Why?"

"G is her older brother."

My eyebrows raised, but I remembered that I had promised not to freak out so I quickly reeled in my concern.

"Exactly how old is her older brother?"

She bit her lip, refusing to make eye contact with me.

"He's 19."

Oh good god.

"19, Bel?!? That's 3 years older than you. Hell, that's illegal! And gross! He should not be dating someone so much younger than him."

Her eyes snapped back at me. "You said you weren't going to freak out!"

"Well, yeah, but that was before I knew you were dating a child predator."

"Excuse me?"

"Bel, I'm sorry, but it's not okay. Not only is he your friend's brother...I mean, does Siena even know about it? But he's also way too old for you."

"No, she doesn't know, and you're not going to tell her or anyone. Right?"

"Bel, I won't tell anyone if you promise to stop seeing him. It's just not a safe situation. He's taking advantage of you."

"You know nothing about him, Maggie. I'm not going to stop seeing him. And you're not going to tell anyone. I told you this in confidence, and if it gets out, I'll know it was you. And I'll never forgive you."

I lowered my head in disappointment. She was putting me in an impossible situation.

"Bel..."

"Just stop." She cut me off. "I know what I'm doing. I'm not a kid anymore. Gianni is a good guy, Maggie. You have nothing to worry about."

I could guarantee you any guy who was "dating" an underage girl and saw no issue with it was far from a "good guy."

But Bel wasn't my sister. We weren't related. It wasn't my place to try to control her or tell her what to do. I tried, but it got to a point where I just couldn't argue with her anymore.

"Okay. I just want you to be safe. Thank you for trusting me with this."

I remember what it was like to be 16 and think every guy was super sweet and interested in you for you. And it was an absolutely magical feeling to be desired at that age, so I couldn't blame her. I was just really worried.

Bel set her arm on the table, palm up. I placed my hand in hers, and she squeezed it tightly. "Thank you, Maggie."

She released my hand and sat back in her chair, letting out a deep sigh. It seemed like she had been waiting to get that off her chest for a while. That was a pretty big secret to carry on your own.

We finished lunch and headed home. There wasn't much talking the entire way back. The silence was needed.

I spent the car ride trying to decide whether to keep my promise to Bel or tell August. We told each other literally everything. I couldn't imagine keeping this from him.

Should I trust her judgement? Should you ever trust a sixteen-year-old's judgement? What did she need most from me?

An ally.

And there it was. Bel needed an ally, a friend. Just like Nic had needed a friend to continue growing as a person. And that was my job: to be her friend. And friends don't break promises. But friends also protect each other.

How could I do both?

I didn't know, but I was determined to find a way.

Nobody said *friendship* was easy.

CHAPTER FOURTEEN

One night, at the very end of the summer, August invited a handful of people over to the house when Fran and Leone were in the US.

Bel was staying at a friend's house for the night, and Nic was out somewhere with Jack and Elliott so August had taken the liberty of turning the house into the closest thing to a fraternity party I'd seen in quite a while.

August ignored me for the majority of the night, and there was only one other girl invited, who wouldn't leave her boyfriend's side the entire time, so I decided to take it easy on the drinking. There was no point in suffering a hangover for a boring night like this.

I spent most of the night on the couch watching a soccer game while the boys played rounds and rounds of beer pong. Trust me, I wouldn't have been watching sports willingly to pass the time. I just couldn't find the freaking remote.

Just when I thought the evening might be, thankfully, wrapping up, the boys erupted in screams as someone came in through the side door. I turned quickly to see who had made such a spectacular entrance.

Lo and behold, it was quite literally the last person in the world I would have wanted to show up. Lucy walked in, feigning embarrassment, wearing tiny white denim shorts and a black crop top that left her entire, perfectly-toned stomach on display.

My eyes were immediately locked on August.

And, speaking of August, did he invite her? I thought they didn't talk.

Or does she just show up randomly? She totally seems like the type of girl who would get wind of a nearby party and turn up uninvited.

August was staring at her with an expression that was somewhere between confused and annoyed as she started making the rounds with the guys. on his face as she began hugging the guysShe started making the rounds with the guys, all of them were lit up with excitement. gave her a brief side hug before passing her onto the next guy. I was pleasantly surprised by the lack of impact her presence seemed to have on him. The others were basically swooning over her, waiting for their turn to get close to her.

She didn't bother coming over to say hi to me, even though we'd made direct eye contact, and I knew she recognized me from that day I saw her with Bel. This girl clearly thinks she has some claim over this family and "the boys," but she couldn't be more wrong. Someday she'll realize that.

August eventually fell asleep sprawled across my lap, and his friends staggered around the living room until they all passed out too, some on couches, most on the floor.

Lucy left, finally, without saying a word to me. Having to constantly sneak glances to locate her throughout the night was getting exhausting. I somehow got August up the stairs. He stopped at the balcony, spreading his arms out wide, mimicking the scene from Titanic.

"Come hold me from behind. I'm the captain of the ship now." I decided to play along. I didn't want to upset him, especially after a night of drinking.

I didn't like it when he was drunk. He had never harmed or threatened me in any way of course, but he just always seemed ready to start an argument or dig up something from the past, typically involving Nic.

I reached around his stomach, holding him tight. He started shouting sloppily. "I will shout it from the rooftops of every building. I'm in love with a girl!" I smiled, resting my head on his back, accepting his drunkenness in return for that cute comment.

"Who's this girl, you ask?" He addressed the imaginary audience below. "Her name is Maggie, Margaret when she needs to be professional, and she is the most beautiful girl in the whole world..."

My smile quickly faded. Before I could even react, he was stumbling away from the railing and into his room. I heard him fall onto his bed.

He called me Margaret. Of course he called me Margaret because I hadn't told him about my name or Gram or the tree or any of it. How had we not yet had that conversation? But Nic and I had?

This literally hit me like a ton of bricks.

My confusion was interrupted by my phone vibrating aggressively in my pocket.

Who the hell was calling me this late? It had to be at least two or three in the morning. Bec or Jen? I checked my phone and didn't recognize the number but could tell it was a local call.

In most situations, I would have just let a random caller go to voicemail, but there was something weird about this.

"Hello?"

"Maggie! Hey! It's Jack!" It took a minute for it to click that it was Nic's friend, Jack. It had been a really long night.

"Jack? Hey, what's up? Everything okay?"

"Um...I'm sorry to call you so late. I got your number out of Nic's phone. I hope that's okay."

"Yeah, that's fine. Is Nic okay?"

"Yeah, he's okay...um...well, sort of. He's been..." The long pause caused me a fit of anxiety.

"He's been crying, Maggie. He's super drunk so that's obviously the reason it's all coming out like this. But he's been going on and on about Ellie and August, but mostly...um...about you. He's in pretty bad shape right now, and I just wondered if you could come get him? I would take him home, but I'm not able to drive right now, and neither is Elliott. Trust me. Do you think you could come?"

I was slightly tempted to tell Jack to just put him to bed and let him sleep it off, but I couldn't go to bed knowing he was that upset, especially if it had anything to do with me.

"Yeah, I can come. Where are you guys?"

"We're at Elliott's. How fast can you get here?"

His tone worried me. I hadn't hung around Jack that often, but every time I had, he was always so easy-going. I'd never heard him be so serious.

"Uh, I'll leave right now. I should be there in like 10, okay?"

"Perfect. See you soon. Maggie?"

"Yeah, Jack?"

"Thank you." He sounded incredibly grateful for such a small favor.

"Don't mention it. I'll be there soon." I shoved the phone back in my pocket, walked down the hall, and peaked my head into August's room to make sure he was asleep. He was snoring softly.

I rushed down the stairs, grabbed the keys to the Jeep, and hustled out to the car. I didn't even worry about August waking up and questioning where I was. I just moved as fast as possible to get to Nic.

I had felt a bit nervous driving the Jeep ever since the accident. I drove slow and steady to avoid any problems.

Luckily, the drive to Elliott's was pretty much a straight shot down the gravel road and a few left turns. I'd been there twice, both times to drop Elliott off after a drunken night at the vineyard.

I only made one wrong turn, an extra left, and, after retracing my steps, soon was pulling into Elliott's driveway. The Jeep's headlights flashed bright on a bunch of kids I'd never met sitting outside around a bonfire that was just about to die out, each one with a lit cigarette in hand.

I pulled up to the side of the house and got out of the car. I left it running, hoping this would be a quick mission, in and out. I approached the fire pit, and everyone stared at me silently.

"Hey, I'm here to pick up Nic. Jack called me."

Two of the girls giggled and whispered something in Italian to each other. There were three other guys, two of whom continued to stare at me silently, and one who pointed toward the front door.

"Thanks."

I entered the house, which was unlocked, and did a quick scan of the space before locking eyes with Jack, who was standing in the kitchen speaking very quietly to Elliott. The scene looked intense.

"Maggie, hey! Thanks for coming. Um...I'm not sure...he came through here not too long ago but I don't know if he went up or down...I'll help you find him."

"Alright," I said, looking around.

"I'll check upstairs. Why don't you check the basement?" He was already heading up the stairs when I nodded. It took me quite a while to find the door to the basement. I asked two people and both of them just stared at me like I was an alien.

Finally, I opened the right door and found clusters of people huddling on the basement stairs. I snaked my way down, swatting my hand through the clouds of smoke in an attempt to see even a few feet in front of me.

I saw a couch with two figures on it. I squinted and moved toward it. It was Nic, who looked to be completely passed out, with a girl straddling his lap and kissing his neck. I rushed over.

"Jesus, get the fuck off him. He's not even awake. What's wrong with you?" I grabbed her arm and pulled her off of him. She gasped and started yelling at me in Italian. I didn't need a translator to know exactly what she was saying.

She gave me a sturdy shoulder check as she passed me.

Jesus, they didn't tell me he was completely passed out.

"Nic, come on. You have to get up. Let's go."

I was reaching my head around his neck, trying to prop him up. He was way heavier than he looked for being so tall and lean.

"No...let's just stay here. I'm fine. You're fine, come on." His eyes remained closed as he attempted to pull me onto his lap. He thought I was that skank.

"Nic, open your eyes. Please. Come on."

He grabbed my waist tightly.

That was it.

"Nicolo Costelli, get your fucking hands off me right now!"

That did the trick. His eyes opened wide and he looked horrified to see me.

"Mags?"

His voice was soft and confused. He released his grip from me immediately. I stumbled my way into a standing position. Seeing him like this was so sad to me.

"Let's go. We're leaving." I used every ounce of the very little muscle I had to drag him up into a standing position. He was incredibly unsteady.

"What...How are you even here? How did you know I was here?" He was trying to hug me, trying to make up for the pain he had just caused me.

"Questions later, car now." My face was serious and stern. I didn't like bossing people around, but he deserved it. He stared at me then nodded slowly and followed me up the stairs. Jack was coming down; I gave him a deep glare.

"You said he was upset. You didn't say he was on the brink of being comatose. He's a fucking mess, Jack. How could you let him get like this?"

Jack looked at me, dejected and humiliated.

"Maggie, I'm sorry. I didn't even notice him drinking more than usual. We were all just pounding beers together in the kitchen, and I don't know what happened."

I shook my head at him. It was hard to believe that some people were okay with letting their friends get like this. I can't count the number of nights that Bec, Jen, and I would go out to the bar together, and one of us would see our ex or start to not feel good, and we would all decide to go home and just chill. That's what you do for friends; you don't let them get this bad.

"Maggie…" Nic and I were heading to the front door, but I ignored his call for me. "Maggie!" Jack yelled much louder, and I snapped around.

"What?!"

"Is that girl okay?!" He squinted as he pointed over to the living room couch. I could see a girl lying under a large, dark-haired man. He had her wrists pinned above her head; thankfully, all their clothes were still on. I told Nic to stay in the kitchen as I headed for the couple on the couch. He was way too messed up to be helpful right now.

The girl on the couch let out a yelp. It wasn't a yelp of pleasure;

she was definitely in pain.

Oh my god. It was Bel.

"Get the fuck off her!" I was hysterical. I grabbed his arms, trying to pull him off of her..

Bel looked so different. She had on dramatic, black eyeliner, and her hair was a tangled mess.

This had to be Gianni, the "good guy."

"Fuck off." He attempted to pin her down again.

Oh, hell no.

I yanked his shoulder as hard as I could, and he fell back onto the other side of the couch. He seemed shocked by my strength, which gave me a few extra seconds to help Bel up to a seated position. She was beyond wasted, even worse than her brother who was standing 10 feet away. She was fighting me, resisting my grip.

"Bel, it's me. It's Maggie. You're okay, come on. We're going to go home now."

"Go away. Doesn't one of my brothers need you for something?"

She's drunk. She's just drunk. I refused to be offended or affected by anything either of these Costelli's drunkenly said to me right now.

Just as I slid my hands under her armpits to try and lift her up, I was shoved to the side, landing hard on the floor.

"She said to go away." Gianni stood over me, sneering. I tried to sit up and immediately started to get dizzy. As Gianni lay back down on Bel, another figure was suddenly towering over them.

"Hey, dick face. Feel good about hurting a girl? Well trust me, this isn't going to feel quite as good." Nic pulled him off Bel with both hands and then punched him squarely in the jaw, way harder than I had seen him punch August during their fight. Gianni fell flat onto the ground.

"Sorry for leaving you lying there, Mags. I just had to do that."

As upset as I still was at him, I had to admit...that was pretty badass.

"Bel, get up. We're leaving." Nic grabbed her arm and started leading her to the door. She didn't fight him.

The car ride home was pretty quiet, to my surprise.

Bel got out of the car first. She stopped at my window before going inside.

"Can you...not tell Fran about this?"

I looked at her with disappointment and slowly nodded my head. Even though tonight was horrible, telling Fran would only make it worse. I opened my door when Nic said, "Wait."

I continued to get out of the car. I wasn't in the mood to talk to him. People say anything when they're drunk.

"I don't want to talk to you. Let's go."

"Maggie, please. I just need a minute."

I reluctantly climbed back into the car and closed the door.

"What! What could you possibly have to say?!" I shouted at him.

"I'm over her. I am. I don't love her anymore. You can't love a dead person. I can't, you can't, like, that's the easy part." I was doing my best to comprehend. "It's not about loving her anymore; it's about me now. It's about figuring out how to forgive myself for falling in love with someone that isn't her."

I refused to turn my head. I couldn't look at him right now. I kept my gaze forward on the side of the house. Maybe he wouldn't even remember this in the morning.

"Mags, look at me. Please." He slid his hand slowly across the center console of the car, reaching for my hand and carefully intertwining his fingers with mine.

"Don't." I tried to pull my hand out of his, but he just gripped tighter.

"I know it's scary to admit it to yourself, but it's just me and you, and we're here together, and you don't have to hide your feelings."

Was I hiding my feelings?

I mean, of course I had feelings for Nic. We had a deep connection. We'd shared so much of ourselves with each other, and he knew all about Gram and my name and the tree...he knew the real me. And, yes, there had been a couple moments where things could have gotten romantic, but they didn't. Because I'm with August.

"Damn it Magnolia, I am trying to tell you that I'm in love with you. Can't you just look at me?"

I thought I was somewhat in control of the situation until he said this. Nic had called me Magnolia hundreds of times before. Ever since I'd told him about Gram, he pretty much exclusively called me that. And it made me smile every single time.

And, for some reason, hearing him say it again made me question everything.

I couldn't blame August for calling me Margaret; I'd never told him the story. It was my fault for not allowing him to get to know that part of me.

Why did I tell Nic and not August?

When I told him, I hadn't even thought twice about it. It just felt effortless, like...he was meant to know.

I was studying him now.

I needed to shut this down.

"Nic, you're a mess. And you've been sleeping with every girl in town all summer. Hell, I just had to drag a girl off of you, and you weren't even awake. This is not fair for you to drop on me, especially not like this, when you're barely coherent."

"Don't you dare try and diminish this. Yeah, Mags, I'm fucked up right now, but I've also never seen things clearer. I just finally got the guts to do something about it." He moved closer to me, much too close.

"You think I've enjoyed those pointless one night stands, the random girls who don't even know my name in the morning? You think that's fun for me? I'm not a monster for trying to find a way to numb the pain of watching you with my brother every single goddamn day." I could hear the hurt in his voice.

His hand let go of mine and moved up to my cheek.

We were no more than a few inches apart now and my heart was racing. I tried to keep looking down, afraid that making eye contact would be the end for me and the last ounce of will-power I had left.

"Nic, we can't. I can't. August is right inside. I can't do this to him."

"But you want to," he said, lifting my chin to force me to look at him. "I know you want to. You're dying to say it too."

"Even if I wanted to say it, I wouldn't. I love August. I really do, and I love you as a best friend. Nic, don't ruin this. Please." His fingers were still holding my chin up.

"Fine. You don't have to say it, not now at least. But you will someday. I'll wait as long as it takes, Magnolia. I will wait for you." He paused, taking a deep breath. "But there is one thing I won't wait for any longer." Before I had a second to pull away, he was kissing me. And I was kissing him.

Nic kissed me hard and slow. He took his time, like the entire thing was strategic and planned and the most important thing in the world. So different from kissing August who was always so breathless and eager.

Finally, he pulled away, and we sat there looking at each other for what seemed an eternity. I couldn't speak. I felt a sense of deep loss, almost grief.

Without a word, we exited the car. Once inside the house, we made our way upstairs. When we reached the top, Nic took my hand and kissed it. I tried to smile but started tearing up instead.

I looked into his eyes one last time before slowly turning away and opening the door to my room. Everything...and I mean *everything* had just changed.

CHAPTER FIFTEEN

The next morning, I woke up next to August who was incredibly hung over and possessed very little knowledge of last night.

I knew I should tell him. About everything. The magnolia tree, my name, but mostly about the horrible mistake I'd made last night with Nic.

August and Nic had patched things up after quarantine was lifted. They'd both apologized sincerely. August had told Nic that he was way out of line for what he'd said about Ellie, and Nic had told August that the whole thing was his fault because he shouldn't have told the family about us to begin with.

If I told August that Nic and I had kissed, the whole mess would start all over. How could I do that to him, to them?

Not to mention the fact that there was a tiny part of me, deep down, that feared it wasn't a mistake.

God, I just needed a break from all the Costelli's.

I told August, who was still half-asleep, that I was going to go for a walk outside to get some fresh air, and he didn't fight me at all.

I walked out to the lake with a steaming coffee mug and sat down by the edge of the water. I stared out onto the horizon, remembering the first time I'd been out there.

So much had happened since then. I felt like a completely different person since I arrived here months ago. Sitting there, it was almost impossible to imagine saying goodbye to this place, these people, and returning to my completely average life. This place had become more like home to me than the place where I spent 20 years growing up.

I could feel tears forming in my eyes, but I was determined to try to focus on the positives. I was so lucky to have been given this opportunity and to have met all these incredibly special people. Who knew a global virus, which had caused so much havoc and trauma across the world, would have an itty bitty silver lining for a girl like me. Yes, that's what I needed to think about, not the absolute mess I had made of my love life.

Sometimes, when life is at its very peak, and we think nothing can get better than this moment right here, right now, we try and hold onto it. We clutch it tightly in order to keep it safe and close. But memories can begin to crumble under that pressure. I closed my eyes and tried to mentally release my tight grip on this place. I wanted to be fully present and soak it all in for, potentially, the last time.

I sat out there for an hour trying to commit every sound, sight, and smell to memory. I was starting to feel nostalgic for a place I hadn't even left yet.

Fran and Leone got home from the airport later that night so we decided to have one last family dinner together, Costelli style. August was leaving tomorrow afternoon on a flight back to London.

He was an admissions leader for the University of London, which meant that he had to go back earlier than everyone else to be there to welcome the new freshman class.

He was the perfect person for the job, warm and funny, just how he had been when I first arrived at the vineyard. We were completely different people then, unaware of how important we would eventually become to each other.

I had no idea how we were going to make this work, dating across an ocean. But August claimed that he would come see me in Michigan every six weeks or so, and we were hoping that I'd be able to go to London every so often.

I knew my parents wouldn't be funding those trips, and I highly doubted a job at the campus bookstore was going to provide me with sufficient funds to fly across the world, but I was still somehow hopeful.

Dinner that night was perfect. We all drank copious amounts of red wine. Fran even allowed Bel to have a glass. Leone got tipsy! I couldn't believe my eyes, but he actually looked like he was having fun. This was the happiest I'd seen everyone in the house in a long time, and it was so bittersweet. We all shared stories about the best parts of the summer and joked about how nervous and shy I was when I had first arrived.

I glanced at August with hope in my eyes that we could make this work, that the distance wouldn't ruin us and the relationship we'd spent all summer building. I was hoping that this could be my second family forever. He looked back at me with the same gorgeous eyes he'd looked at me with that night at the club in Florence, convincing me with absolutely no words that his love for me was real.

August left early the next morning. He woke me up, and I walked him down to the end of the driveway while he waited for his taxi to arrive. There wasn't much talking. He just held me, and I cried. A lot. He kissed my forehead and looked me in the eyes.

"I love you. We will be okay."

I nodded, trying to believe him.

"I love you too."

I had decided not to go to the airport with him. I refused to be that character in all the rom-com movies who just stands there pathetically as the person they love walks away. I always wanted to shake the TV and scream, "Don't let them leave! We all know you're going to regret it like three scenes from now!"

But when you're actually in the situation, saying goodbye isn't romantic at all. It's gut-wrenching and terrifying when you don't know when you'll get to see that person again. All the memories you'd made together flash in your head as you kiss them for the last time, surrendering to the idea that things probably won't ever be the same.

After August left in the taxi, I decided to walk down to the lake one last time before I left the next day. At least out there nobody would hear me crying.

I made my way through the trees and saw that someone had beat me to it. Nic was sitting at the edge of the water, pulling at individual pieces of grass.

"I should've known I'd find you out here. Best view of the sunrise." I sat down next to him. He glanced over at me and back down to the grass. A shy smile emerged on his face.

"You know, I'm not sure exactly when it happened, but recently, I've been able to watch the sun come up and not feel sad. I used to sit out here and just cry. Every sunrise I watched was one that she didn't get to see. But now, I don't know. It's different. Each one just reminds me that I get another day, another chance."

"Suffering can open our hearts and allow us to see things differently."

"I wanted to thank you, Mags. For always being there for me. And for seeing past the mask I wore for so long. Nobody had the courage to crack me open and help me face my own worst enemy: myself. You taught me that grief isn't something I had to hide, and once I realized that, I allowed myself to actually feel it all. Which helped me understand it better. I couldn't have done it without you."

"I'm so glad, Nic. You deserve to be happy. You never have to hide parts of yourself from me."

He turned his entire body to face me now.

"I wish you weren't leaving, Mags. This place..." He looked out onto the water. "It won't be the same without you."

I scooted closer to him and grabbed him for a hug. He embraced me and wrapped his arms around my lower back tightly.

"I'll be back," I whispered in his ear.

He pulled away from the hug and looked directly in my eyes. He stared at me for a few seconds before he kissed my forehead.

If it were anyone other than Nic, I would have been weirded out by it. But it felt nice with him, comforting, and I really needed that right now.

"I'll be waiting, Magnolia."

CHAPTER SIXTEEN

Two Years Later

August 2022

When I got back to the US after that...whirlwind...of a summer, COVID-19 was still raging on here. People were starting to grow tired of living their lives inside and basically giving up on the quarantine thing. The amount of snapchat and Instagram stories I would see of people I knew at crowded bars and restaurants, all while case and death numbers were rising daily...it was just sickening.

Especially because I had a close family member, my sister-in-law Carissa, who wasn't able to see Derek for months at a time because the risk was too high with her working in the hospital. People are so damn selfish.

But luckily, we eventually got things under control. A vaccine was finally developed and approved by the FDA, people were really nervous to take it at first. All these ridiculous conspiracy theories about government microchipping...as if we aren't all willingly pressing our fingerprints into our smart phones every day.

I'm not sure if the world will ever fully recover though. People still wear masks to the grocery store. There will be random flare ups here and there, especially during flu season. I think that fear will always live with us, as the whole thing was quite traumatic.

I graduated college a semester early last December, which was shocking considering I basically stopped trying after I got home from the vineyard. Taking graduation pictures during a Michigan December was strange, but somehow still perfect. The snow was falling on my green grad cap, and it honestly made the pictures that much better.

I couldn't blame my lack of academic motivation entirely on my Italian adventure, but it definitely played its part...along with August and I breaking up. Yeah, I was just as shocked as you.

August had kept his promise. He came to visit every six weeks. Since I was still in school, I couldn't just up and leave for London, not that I had the money anyway, so he carried the slack and made the effort to come here.

He met my family and my friends, and life was really great. I really thought we could make the long distance thing work until we could figure out which one of us would make the big move across the ocean.

After he graduated, he got a job as a production assistant for a local news channel in London. He completely threw himself into his work, trying to impress his bosses and convince them he was dedicated to advancing in the field.

But the cost of his hard work was lack of attention to his girlfriend. I tried to be understanding about his new and exciting job. I even made a schedule of times we could FaceTime each other, making sure it perfectly corresponded with his work, gym, and social calendar.

But it wasn't enough.

We were fighting a lot and finally took a "break," which I think we can all agree is just a code word for the breakup that happens before the actual breakup.

For Christmas last year, my dad had bought me a plane ticket to go visit August. I didn't have the heart to tell him about our break so I just accepted the gift graciously. But after thinking it over, I thought a surprise visit might be just what our relationship needed. A kick in the butt. A little spontaneity. So I decided to pull out the best romantic gesture I could think of and surprise him.

I had his address so I decided to just show up on his doorstep. Maybe this last-ditch effort would be enough to save us and get us back on track.

When I arrived, I buzzed his apartment, and a not-so-manly voice responded.

"August's flat, who is it?" My heart shattered at the sound of the voice. I almost threw up right there.

How fucking stupid was I for flying all the way here, just to find out that it wasn't his job keeping him busy this entire time, it was her. This random girl on the other side of the intercom that I wanted to strangle.

"Sorry, wrong flat." That's all I could get out before bursting into tears. I ran down the steps and out onto the street where I hailed the first cab I saw. I got on the next flight back to the US.

To this day, 9 or so months later, I still haven't told August I ever flew to London to see him for Christmas. I was so humiliated and dejected that I didn't even want to bring it up.

When I got back home, I told him that I thought we should make the break a permanent break-up. He barely fought me on it, which made me want to bring up the spontaneous trip to London even less. It didn't matter; we were done. I was done. It was time to move on.

Fran and I often talked on the phone. She would tell me about all the events they were planning and any new business. I loved that she kept me "in the loop."

Their wine had officially launched in the US last year and I bought it for all my friends right when it hit the shelves. I couldn't tell you how many bottles Bec, Jen, and I have drunk. Whenever I see the label it always brings back vivid memories of my crazy time at the vineyard. I still tell Bec and Jen stories of all the wacky stuff that happened at the Costelli's, they keep telling me I should write a book about it.

I also talked to Bel pretty frequently as she was starting to look into colleges and trying to decide whether to go somewhere in Italy or elsewhere. She had a million questions about colleges in the U.S. I always ended up telling her I thought she would fit right in. American colleges would love her. I really hoped she would come to the U.S. for college because I missed her like crazy. She was dying to visit me to see where I lived, but mostly, she wanted to see Lake Michigan, which made me so happy.

Sometime late last January, I received my first letter from Nic. We hadn't talked since I left the vineyard. When I pulled the envelope out of my mailbox, I was so shocked that I just stood there looking at it. While my heart did a happy dance.

The first letter he sent was pretty short, mainly just an update on his life.

I wrote back, of course. I told him about graduation and adjusting back to American life...I didn't mention that August and I had officially broken up; I was pretty sure someone else had told him.

After the first four or five letters, we started writing to each other often, like every week. Our letters got longer and longer. We started sharing more details about our lives, and, eventually, spoke about anything and everything.

When I was expecting a letter from him, I would find myself checking my mailbox way too often, and if the letter didn't come, it would kind of ruin my day .

Sometimes he would include pictures of the family; even Jack and Elliott would sometimes sneak their way into the envelope with his updates. In one letter, he enclosed the disposable photo he had taken of me when I tripped on the vines that first week on the vineyard. Holding the picture between my fingers, I laughed softly to myself. I couldn't believe that it was from only a couple years ago. It felt like a lifetime.

We purposely didn't communicate by text or email or phone -- just letters. He had told me that he loved knowing that my hands would touch the same paper he was writing on. He also said that writing down stuff about his life and knowing that I would read it helped him in those moments when he got down on himself.

I loved both of those sentiments so I was happy to write. And, honestly, old-fashioned letters are kind of romantic.

Then, all of a sudden, his letters stopped. It had now been nine weeks. I wanted to reach out and ask what happened and why he wasn't writing anymore, but the thought of groveling like that made me feel pathetic. I was sure someone would have told me if something bad had happened.

I was pretty depressed that first month with no letters. No, I was very depressed. Maybe, just like with August, someone new and exciting had come along and caught his attention. So much for my hands touching the same paper as his.

I'll be waiting, Magnolia.

I missed him. *A lot.*

I had been working at a local coffee shop ever since I graduated. It wasn't my dream job, and certainly not the job I thought I'd get freshly out of a highly acclaimed school like Michigan State, but it was okay for now.

Bec and Jen had BOTH decided to get their Master's degrees straight out of undergrad, which shouldn't have come as a shock at all. But, luckily for me, they stayed at Michigan State for grad school so I was able to see them pretty often.

The coffee shop I worked at was owned by an adorable couple, June and Levi. He opened it for her because of her love for all things coffee. They named the shop Java June, which I thought had the most charming ring to it. Levi mainly worked on maintenance stuff around the shop while June was the brains of the operation.

We were currently in the middle of moving the entire shop to a new location. I was working my butt off, mostly driving stuff to the new location and just trying to get it ready. It was a ton of work, but I really loved and respected my bosses and honestly just wanted to be a great employee to them. And, you never know; maybe with more customers, the shop would expand, and I could create my dream job there. Stranger things have happened.

It struck me one day while I was sweeping the floor in our new location that the way I thought about work, any kind of work, had changed. Doing work, whether it was a job, or school work, or a chore at home...it used to feel pointless, disconnected from my real life, like it was something extra to just not want to do. But now...I think about work as something that moves you toward good things, that has a purpose. Sooner or later. Pretty sure it was my time at the vineyard that taught me that.

I drove to the shop early one day, thinking I'd surprise Levi and June by getting a head start on the painting we desperately needed to do. I was just about to dip my brush into the paint when the front door opened.

I quickly looked up to see who had just entered our clearly under-construction storefront, thinking maybe Levi and June had shown up earlier than expected.

"Oh, shit. Sorry. You're not open yet, are you?"

I looked at the (tall, blonde, handsome, and in scrubs) man and then back at the completely empty space surrounding me.

Was he joking?

"No sir. Sorry! We won't be open for a month or so. Shooting to be ready by orientation week."

"Damn it." He slumped down onto the floor. Like, he sat on the floor. "Ma'am, I don't think you understand. I will die without coffee." He was holding his head in his hands.

Ma'am?

I stared at him. What do you say to that?

"Um...I'd really like to help you, but, unfortunately, I can't, so... there are a few other coffee shops down the street, though. I'm sorry I can't help."

"I see. Well, then, you're just going to have to make it up to me, Miss..." He jumped up energetically.

I looked at him blankly, shaken by his audacity.

"This is the part where you tell me your name."

I laughed quietly. "Actually, this is the part where I unfortunately have to get to work. As you can see, there's a lot of painting to get done so we can open and serve the...passionate...coffee lovers like you."

He cocked his head like I had just insulted him.

"I refuse to leave until I know your name, sassy little barista lady." He crossed his arms.

I rolled my eyes with a smile and took a deep breath. "Fine. My name is Magnolia. And I'm not a barista."

I had started introducing myself with my real, full name. I mean, why not? It made me happy every time I heard it. I realized that I'd been holding on to it too tightly. Now I wanted to share it.

"But I really do need to get back to work."

"Well, then, let's stop talking and get painting."

Did he just say, "let's?"

Because...hell no.

"Um...what are you doing?"

"I'm holding up my end of the deal." He had grabbed a brush and was dipping it into the paint can. I was literally standing there looking at him with my mouth open. He started painting the higher areas I couldn't reach. He had to be at least 6'3". And was built like an athlete. Not that I was looking or anything.

"And what deal is that?"

"I help you finish painting, and you get coffee with me down the street at one of those places you mentioned."

Oh my god.

"Thank you, but...I have to work all day."

He stopped painting and looked back at me. His piercing blue eyes peeked out from under his long, dirty blond hair. He smiled for the first time since entering the shop.

Hm...handsome. Strange, but handsome.

"Well then, Magnolia, the deal's off."

He was still smiling as he set the paintbrush on the top of the can. Why do I keep getting myself into these sexually charged painting situations with attractive men?

"It was my pleasure to make your acquaintance today, Magnolia."

He grabbed his bag off the floor and opened the door before looking back at me briefly.

"I'll be seeing you soon."

After he left, I stood there staring at the door still trying to comprehend what had just happened. I mean, it had to be said, the man was absolutely beautiful. And obviously worked at the hospital or did something medically related. But he was also so intrusive and arrogant and way, way too sure of himself. Funny in a weird way. Kind of reminded me of *someone*.

Levi and June showed up about an hour later and were thrilled with the results of my hard work. After we finished for the day, they treated me to dinner down the street at the local Mexican restaurant.

I decided not to tell them about the stranger who had strolled into the store today and briefly taken over my life. They didn't need one more thing to be concerned about.

We headed back to the shop so I could grab my stuff and drive home. I told them they could go and that I would lock up.

After they were gone, I stood in the empty shop and looked around. There was still so much left to do; I wasn't sure it would be physically possible to finish in just a little over a month. Before I knew it, I was pouring out a container of paint so I could do a little more before I drove back home. Doing a little more turned into doing a lot more. I worked until about midnight.

I opened up my messages to my dad and typed: "Staying in East Lansing for the night. Be home tomorrow. XO."

My dad was definitely already asleep, but I didn't want him to wake up tomorrow and worry about where I was or why I hadn't come home.

Living with just my dad had been working out pretty well,

actually. When I graduated, I didn't have enough money to even consider living on my own. I knew my dad would be happy to spend more time with me, and, thankfully, he graciously offered a room in his condo to me, rent free.

I hadn't kept in super close contact with Mom since graduating, but she and Roger were thoughtful enough to send me $100 in the mail with a dollar store card that read: "ConGRADulations!"

Very original, I know.

I hit send on the message to dad and plugged my phone into the charger. I locked the front door and turned off the main lights.

June had already brought a small couch into her office space. I wandered in to see if I could make it work for a quick nap. It was the perfect size for me. I didn't have a blanket or a pillow, but I was too tired to care.

I had only planned to sleep for a few hours so I could keep working and surprise Levi and June tomorrow when they came in. I quickly dozed off to the faint sound of Nickelback from the tattoo parlor next door.

The next morning I woke up to a banging sound.

Oh, no. Oh, no no no.

I'd slept way longer than I'd intended to. I quickly hopped up off the couch to investigate the noise coming from the front of the store. It was still partially dark so I squinted to find my way.

I saw a tall figure knocking on the door.

Who the hell would be here this early?

Did Levi forget his set of keys? What...what time even is it?

They're going to be so pissed that I stayed here overnight. I started to scramble and fix my hair before opening the door, praying it wasn't going to be my boss on the other side.

I slowly pulled the door open.

Oh my god.

"Good morning, Magnolia!"

You've got to be joking.

The strange, sexy man from yesterday pushed right past me and flipped the light switch on like he owned the damn place.

"Wh...What the hell are you doing here?" I could barely open my eyes against the bright fluorescent lights. I put my hand up as a shield. I was definitely not yet fully awake. Was I dressed?

"I come bearing gifts." He held a coffee carrier in each hand. Each one contained four cups of coffee. I surveyed all of it and then looked at him blankly. It suddenly crossed my mind how smudged I must look. And why did he have so much coffee?

"You told me to go to the other coffee shops down the street, so I did. You said there were a few; turns out there were only a couple: The Urban Cup and Schuler Books and Music. Both were charming in their own way. And you also said you wouldn't go have coffee with me, so I brought...the coffee...to you. Now, as you can see, not knowing your preference of course, I have brought, from each of the two coffee shops that is, four options: black, cream only, cream and sugar, and sugar only." As he listed them, he pointed to each option.

I was trying to work out whether I was more annoyed that he had woken me up, stunned at what he had just done, or simply grateful for the coffee. Regardless, I was in no position to reject free coffee, none at all, not even from this extremely bizarre person.

I grabbed the cup of black coffee from the Urban Cup carrier and took a long, heavenly sip.

"How did you know I'd be here this early?"

"Well, I didn't set up a tent and sleep outside the shop all night, if that's what you're suggesting," he said with a completely straight face.

I laughed drowsily at his goofy humor. "Obviously, I wasn't suggesting that."

"Well, this establishment just so happens to be on my route to the hospital, and I remembered you saying you needed to get a lot more work done. You seemed like a very determined gal, so I took my chances."

"Plus," he added, "I had to see you again or I was going to die. It's a medical condition. I'm a doctor so I would know."

He was so ridiculous and hysterical. And a doctor. A doctor with distractingly blue eyes and pretty fucking incredible arms.

"A doctor, huh?"

"Well, technically, a resident. I went to school here for undergrad. Number 17!" He gave a fist pump.

I looked at him calmly as I took another sip of the free coffee. Was I supposed to know what number 17 meant?

"On the football team. I was number 17 on the football team."

He didn't quite seem to read my disinterest in the topic.

"Not a big sports gal," I said, wondering if he would get that I was mocking his use of the word, "gal."

"What kind of gal are you then?"

Yeah, he got it.

He pulled out the "sugar only" cup of coffee from the Schuler Books and Music carrier and took a long sip. Before I could even think about answering the question, he chimed in again.

"Other than being a determined, intelligent, radiant, non-barista, impossible-to-flirt-with gal?"

He was good.

And crazy hot.

And a doctor, *for god's sake.*

But...

I knew guys like him. Guys who didn't take no for an answer. Guys whose assertiveness can cross over to aggression really fast. Guys who act like you're "the one" from the second they see you. Guys who seem so charming and perfect; that is, until they don't.

In fact, I had known one of those guys very, very well. I fell in love with that guy. And he broke my heart.

I couldn't go through all that again.

It wasn't that I was still hung up on August, but the whole experience with him had taken so much out of me emotionally.

Maybe I wasn't being fair to this guy. I obviously barely knew him. But the fact was: he was doing all the stuff August did at the beginning. All the over-the-top stuff.

And suddenly, my brain went to Nic.

This guy wasn't Nic.

I don't want another August. I just can't.

"Well, I'm a busy gal! And you know what, can we stop saying gal, please?"

"Fine, no more gal, just Magnolia from now on."

"And you should probably get to work, and so should I. Thank you for the coffee. It really was kind of you, but I have so much to do and, to be frank, you're distracting me."

I felt sort of rude turning him down like this. But this was what was best for now.

It was good for guys like this to be told no every once in a while anyway. They were so used to getting their way and having girls fall at their feet. I was doing him a favor, actually.

He pulled out a pen from his coat pocket and scribbled something quickly on the side of his coffee cup. He set it down right in front of me, shot me a quick grin, and left through the front door without another word.

I couldn't help it; I walked over and grabbed the cup, twisting it in my hand to see his writing. Written in perfect handwriting:

Have dinner with me. I'll die if you don't.
345-789-2334
Wyatt

It wasn't until then that I realized he had never told me his name. Wyatt. I said it over and over in my head. It didn't really fit him, but I still liked the name. I leaned up against June's desk, held up the cup, and stared at his dramatic invitation. I slowly traced his phone number with my thumb. Something was nagging at me. Was I being unfair to him by not even giving him a chance?

No. I was taking care of myself.

I tossed the cup in the trash before turning off the light and leaving for home.

When Levi and June showed up that afternoon, they were overwhelmingly grateful for the amount of time and effort I'd put in. Levi almost cried seeing how the place was finally coming together. It was so adorable seeing how much he wanted it to be special for June. They gave me the rest of the afternoon off and slid me a $20 bill to grab lunch before I headed home. They really were way too generous to me.

I headed out of the shop and wandered down the street to a nearby sandwich cafe. I grabbed a pre-made turkey wrap from the refrigerated section. I was dying to get home, and I was just too tired to wait for a real meal. I paid for my lunch with the money Levi and June had given me and dug in my bag for my phone.

Shit.

I must've left it charging in June's office.

I swung my bag back over my shoulder and took a bite of my wrap before heading back to the shop. The front door was locked when I got back. I guessed that they had slipped out for lunch. I opened the door with my keys and made my way to the office to grab my phone and charger. I pushed the door open to the office and flipped on the light switch. Immediately, something on June's desk caught my attention.

The same coffee cup I had thrown out this morning sat on the corner of the desk. It rested on top of a bright pink sticky note.

Oh no.

They must've found it and thought I was having some boy come into the shop when they weren't here. This was not good. I rushed over to the cup and lifted the note out from under it.

You don't want his death on your conscience ! And we need you here to work, not in jail! Dinner won't hurt. Call him and have fun.

Xoxo,
June

June wasn't mad, thank god. I took a deep breath.

Closing my eyes, my thoughts ran to Gram.

What would she think of all this? Who am I kidding? I knew exactly what she would think.

She wouldn't tell me what to do. She would ask how I felt, and we would talk about it until I finally admitted that I was afraid. Afraid of being hurt again. And then she would say something incredibly wise like, "The opposite of fear is love, my darling. Always choose love."

I flipped the sticky note over and wrote down Wyatt's phone number. I folded it up and threw it in my bag. I threw away the cup (again) and locked up the shop on my way out to the car.

On the drive home, I couldn't stop thinking about that damn note in my bag.

Maybe one dinner wouldn't hurt; it was free food after all.

I pulled into the driveway, put the car in park, and retrieved the pink sticky note from my bag. I stared at June's writing, then flipped it over and stared at his number, then June's writing, then his number.

This cycle went on for about 5 minutes before I finally picked up my phone and decided to go for it.

What's the worst that could happen? I felt a surge of courage and recklessness flood through me, the same feeling I'd had that day I decided to stay in Italy indefinitely. I dialed the number and became less and less confident with each ring.

He's not going to answer.

He already changed his mind. I'm such an idiot.

"Hello?"

"Oh, uh, hi. I didn't think you were going to answer."

He paused. "Well, I didn't think you were going to call."

Bullshit.

He knew I was going to call. Any girl would call.

"I almost didn't. My boss, actually…She, uh, convinced me that I couldn't miss work for doing jail time because of your death. So…I'm actually only saying yes so you don't die and so I can keep my job."

"Well, your boss sounds like a smart lady. Tomorrow night. I'll pick you up at the shop at 6:30. The rest is a surprise."

"I'm busy tomorrow night."

"No you're not."

The nerve.

But he was actually right. I wasn't busy. I just didn't think he was going to ask me to dinner that soon. I wasn't ready.

"Fine."

"Fine? That easy?"

"Don't make me change my mind."

"I'll see you tomorrow, gal." He hung up before I could yell at him for calling me that stupid name again.

I threw my phone into my bag and went inside the house. My dad was asleep on the couch tangled up in a blanket, and the TV was way too loud. I grabbed the remote and turned it off; pulled the blanket out from under him and placed it neatly on top of him; and headed to my room for the night.

When I woke up the next morning, I was in full-blown panic mode.

Why the hell did I agree to this?

I can't date. I won't. *I'm not going.*

I pulled my phone off the bedside table and opened the FaceTime app. I put Bec and Jen in a group and hit dial. They both answered quickly, thank god.

"Hi guys."

"Mag, what's up? I'm studying so I can't talk long." Bec slid her glasses up into her hair and propped the phone up so she didn't have to hold it.

"Hey, Maggie!" Jen propped her phone up while pouring Frosted Flakes into a bowl.

"I need your help," I stated bluntly.

Jens eyes lit up with curiosity, but Bec's remained neutral.

"Ooooh, with what?" Jen was instantly intrigued.

"I...sort of..."

"You're pregnant," Bec interrupted.

"Jesus, Bec. No! Who the hell would have gotten me pregnant?"

She shot me a look like that was a stupid question.

"No I'm not pregnant. Not even close. I have a… thing tonight. A…a date."

"Did you just say a date? Bec, did she say a date?" Jen was way more excited about this than I was. At least someone was.

"She did, Jen. Calm down. With whom?"

"Long story. His name is Wyatt. He's a doctor, well, a resident, in East Lansing."

"Oh my god. You're dating a doctor? Yes, Maggie! You go, girl!" Jen was jumping out of her seat at this point.

"How the hell did you meet a doctor when you don't even have time to call your best friends because of your oh-so-busy job?"

Ouch.

I took a cleansing breath.

"He came into work one day. He was…persistent, to say the least."

"Wait…so…what exactly do you need help with? You better not be questioning whether to go or not." Jen's expression was dead-ass serious.

"I actually don't think I should, guys. What if he's a jerk? What if it's awkward?"

"What if this, what if that…we could do this all day, Maggie. You have to get back out there eventually, right? Even if it's terrible…it'll help you know what you don't want."

Count on Bec to make this a perfectly logical argument.

"I agree. You're going. And you're coming over after so you can tell us how it went."

"Jen, did you not hear me saying I have to study?" Bec held up her book and waved it in front of the camera.

"Managerial accounting can wait. The recap of Maggie's date with the doctor, however, cannot. We haven't had a sleepover in forever. This is the perfect opportunity."

I smiled, thinking about us having a girls' night like old times. We really needed that.

Bec was hesitant, but once she saw how excited Jen and I were, she gave in.

"Fine. Text us when you're on your way back, Mag. Have fun, and be safe." She quickly exited off the group call, leaving me and Jen alone.

"I can't wait to see you. I miss you so much."

"I can't wait either, Jen. I'll see you soon. Wish me luck!" I crossed my fingers with one hand and blew her a kiss with the other before ending the call.

I felt so much better. Like Bec had said, even if this failed utterly and completely, which it probably would, I'll be fine and learn from it.

The afternoon quickly escaped me as I attempted to find the right outfit for the night. I needed something that was a step up from the paint-ridden clothes he'd seen me in, but not something that was too try-hard.

I settled on a pair of jeans with a loose, white, off-the-shoulder top. I put my hair up in a ponytail and tied a green paisley hair scarf around it. I added some small, gold hoops and a pair of brown, strappy sandals. I looked at myself in the full-length mirror in the corner of my bedroom one last time. My outfit was casual, but still classy. I did a spin to make sure everything looked okay and grabbed my bag. The nerves were starting to set in.

I made my way out into the living room and found my dad in the same spot as last night. I couldn't help but feel sorry for him. He never left that damn couch.

"I'm heading out for the night, pops. I'm staying at Jen's so don't wait up, okay?"

"Got it. Thanks."

I smiled at him and went to open the door.

"Hey," he shouted. I turned around quickly.

"You look beautiful, Magnolia."

At that moment, I thought my heart would explode. Something about hearing my dad call me by that name made me so happy.

Here goes nothing.

CHAPTER SEVENTEEN

I'd been sitting in June's office for 30 minutes waiting for Wyatt. He was late, of course. And I was sure he'd have some grand excuse about how he had to save some infant's life or something else totally noble and irrefutable. I reached into my purse to check the time, again, and found a missed text from the subject in question.

I'm coming. So sorry. Don't you dare leave.

I rolled my eyes at the text and set my phone down on June's desk without responding. Patience had never been my strong suit. I waited for another 25 minutes, and that was it. I didn't even want to go on this date in the first place, so why would I sit here and wait like a pathetic loser for some guy who probably wouldn't even show up.

I threw my phone into my bag, and stood up. I decided to walk extremely slowly to the door just to give him one last chance to not disappoint me. But I made it all the way to the door and there was still no sign of him. I stepped outside and turned to lock the door.

"I told you not to leave!"

Wyatt had just rounded the corner. He was entirely out of breath. He was wearing a pair of khakis with a navy blue collared shirt and still had his stethoscope around his neck.

Good god. Sexy as hell. *But so late.*

"Yeah, well, you told me to be here at 6:30 and it's now 7:30, so..." I pushed my way past him and the gorgeous bouquet of flowers he was holding.

"Magnolia, wait. Please stop." He rushed in front of me to block my path. "I'm sure you already know why I'm late. I can't help it. It's my job. I tried as hard as I could, but there was a big accident on the expressway. The ER was overflowing." He passed the bouquet to me.

I couldn't be totally heartless about this. Like he said, it was his career. As far as excuses went, this was about the best of the best. I took the bouquet and inhaled the floral scent deeply. Of course they were my favorites: peonies. This bouquet had to be at least $100...I couldn't stop staring at it.

"I really am sorry. This is not how I wanted to start off, but, I promise, what I have planned should make up for it."

He had a large bag hanging over his shoulder, but I couldn't tell what type of activity it was intended for. I just really hoped it wasn't something active. It was hot enough out here, and I was already regretting the choice to wear jeans.

"Where are we going?"

He smiled so big, it lit up the entire block.

"Let's go." He grabbed my hand and led me down the sidewalk.

Here I was, following yet another guy to yet another unknown destination. This was starting to become a bad habit.

We passed a handful of restaurants and bars on our walk, and I wanted desperately to ask why we weren't stopping at any but decided to just go with the flow.

Finally, he led me off the main road, and we entered a small park with tons of benches and people lying on blankets. Once we found an open spot on the grass, he pulled a wool blanket out of his large bag and spread it out on the ground. I smiled at the amount of preparation he had clearly put into this and took a seat.

He sat down next to me. I looked around at all the people seated near us that seemed to also be on dates. This was normal. I kept repeating that in my head.

Dating is good.

Dating is normal.

I continued to survey the park when he pulled a bottle of wine and two plastic glasses out of his bag.

My entire body went into shock. I couldn't even force my arm to grab the cup he was holding out for me. I just stared and stared and stared. Positioned in his lap was a bottle of Costelli Vineyards wine. Even though I couldn't read the name on the label, I could see enough to recognize their logo.

I finally grabbed the cup from him. He poured me a glass as he talked about his chaotic day at work, but I couldn't stop staring at the wine. It wasn't the original bottle they had released in the U.S.; that one was a deep red pinot noir and this, a crisp chardonnay. This must be their newest release.

I took a long sip and just couldn't control what came out of my mouth next.

"This wine is really good. Can I see the bottle? I'm always looking for a good Chardonnay."

He swiftly passed me the bottle, and I turned it to see the label.

My name.

It said my name…in beautiful, blush, cursive letters: "Magnolia," spread right across the front.

"Can you guess why I bought this wine?"

"Yeah, I think I can. That's very sweet."

After I had committed the design to memory and begun to come to terms with the fact that the Costelli's had named a freaking wine after me, I passed the bottle back to him and took a dangerously-long gulp from my glass.

"Looks like someone else had a rough day too." Wyatt laughed as he watched me down my entire cup. I shrugged as he poured me another glass.

"So, you might be thinking this is just an ordinary picnic in the park. But I promise there's still a few more surprises in store. Let's start with what's in my handy dandy bag here." Wyatt reached deep into the bag and pulled out a handful of items.

"So, as a medical student, I've always been a visual learner. I like to see things in order to understand them. So I brought you a few things. I know it's not a traditional dinner…but hopefully this will help you understand me a little better."

Good god.

He was like…an adult. With maturity and thoughtfulness. And

he really wanted us to get to know each other. When he'd asked me to have dinner with him, this wasn't exactly what I'd had in mind. I thought this was going to be an easy one-time date, but boy was I was wrong.

I couldn't complain though; he was really sweet. I smiled as I watched him sort through his items.

"I feel so unprepared now."

"Don't worry. I have other ways I plan to get to know you."

I felt my stomach flip upside down. He was kind of the perfect mix of sexy and considerate. A truly lethal combination.

"Anyway..." He snapped back to his show-and-tell presentation. I was all ears for this. I needed to learn what made this rare man tick.

"First things first. M&Ms." He ripped open the package of pretzel M&Ms, which just so happened to be my absolute favorite, and poured me a handful.

"My dad worked for MARS, the candy company, growing up. We had to move a lot for his job because he was always being transferred. We went from Chicago to New Jersey to Pennsylvania, and the one and only thing that remained constant was my dad's attempt to make us feel better about the constant moving with copious amounts of M&Ms. Like, every flavor you can imagine. It was amazing."

"Pretzel's the best." I snacked on mine. "How'd you end up in Michigan?"

"He was born here and went to Michigan State too. Met my mom in undergrad, so when he retired, they wanted to bring us all back here. I think they strategically wanted us to be closer to

Michigan State so we'd all choose to go to school there too, you know, carry on the legacy. Which we all did, so I guess their tactic worked."

"So what does your mom do?"

"Ah, yes. That brings me to my next items." He pulled out a white plastic container, placing it on the blanket and removing the lid. Inside was a small, green, folded-up towel. He opened up the towel, revealing six golden brown, crescent shaped, hand pies.

"My mom is a pastry chef."

He was looking intently at the pies.

"Let's see...ok, these two are mushroom, gorgonzola, and caramelized onion, and these two are...artichoke, jalapeño, and bacon, this one's blueberry, and this one is lemon." He was pointing at them as he named them just as he had done with the coffees in the shop.

Are you kidding me? Whoever said "the way to a man's heart is through his stomach"...clearly never met a hungry woman.

"Wow. Those look and sound absolutely amazing."

"Yeah. She's worked in restaurants, hotels, even owned her own bakery at one point. But she always found a way to pick up and move wherever my dad needed to go, always adjusting to our new location and finding a way to keep baking. She's the one who taught me the most about compromise and doing whatever it takes to support your partner."

He offered the container of pies to me with a smile. I decided to go with the vegetarian option. Wyatt handed me a napkin.

"Your house must have always smelled so good with your mom

baking all the time." I took a big bite of the pie and almost melted. "This is...so delicious."

"My mom loves to bake for people. Especially pretty girls that I tell her I need to impress." He was blushing. He grabbed one of the pies and took a bite.

He really had his mom make this special for this date. Now I was the one blushing.

"Please tell your mom I said thank you. This is incredible."

"Alright, this is the last one. And, unfortunately, it's not food-related. But this one might be the most important."

I shifted to a more upright position and placed my hand pie on my napkin to demonstrate that I was seriously listening. I could tell whatever he was about to say was super important to him. He handed me a neon green hospital bracelet. I spun it around in my fingers trying to understand its significance.

"My senior year here, I was driving to my very last Homecoming game at the stadium. I was only a quarter of a mile away, and some drunk idiot blew through a red light. He hit my drivers side going 50 miles an hour and flipped the car 3 full times."

He paused like he needed to catch his breath.

"Well, needless to say, I missed the game. And every game for the rest of my senior season. I was in a coma for 2 months. I actually remember hearing the doctor talking with my parents about options if I didn't wake up."

"Wyatt...I'm so sorry."

"Don't apologize. I recovered, luckily, with no real long-term consequences. But the reason I brought that bracelet and the reason

I'm telling you all this is because that's when I decided to go into the medical field. Seeing the joy on my parents' faces when I woke up was something I wanted to witness on a daily basis. I decided I needed to be part of the reason those miracles happen."

"Wow. That is…such a beautiful story, Wyatt."

I held the bracelet out for him to take, but he shook his head.

"Keep it. The day I finally got to take that damn thing off was one of the happiest days of my life." He looked proud to be sharing with me such a big part of himself.

I suddenly flashed back to that first time in the barn with Nic when he told me about Ellie. Wyatt, like Nic, was sensitive and not afraid to be vulnerable. Maybe he wasn't so much like August after all.

I tucked the bracelet neatly in my bag. We finished our pies, and he asked me a few questions about my family. It was starting to get dark.

"Thank you. For the treats and the stories…it's all been wonderful. You're too kind, really."

"Oh, it's not over yet, gal. That was just the first half." He squeezed my hand tightly. Just as I was about to give him a hard time for calling me gal, I noticed that the other couples around us were starting to stand up. But they weren't leaving.

Actually, I think they're dancing?

What the hell is going on?

I looked around, incredibly confused, but Wyatt remained perfectly calm, like he knew exactly what was happening.

"Have you ever been to a silent disco?" He pulled his phone from his pocket.

"A what?"

"A silent disco!" He sounded so excited but I truly had no clue what he was talking about. "Basically, a bunch of people gather like if they were at a concert, except everyone has their own personal concert by wearing headphones and listening to whatever music they like."

We both laughed as we watched some people get incredibly into their moves. It was quite funny to watch.

"So we're going to... dance? Right here in the park?"

"We sure are." He stood up and reached down for my hand. "I made a playlist...with some songs I like that I hope you like too." Once we were both standing, he handed me one of his bluetooth earbuds and placed the other in his ear. Okay, I was not about to dance in front of all these people. I actually refuse.

He pressed play on the playlist and "The Heart of Life" by John Mayer came on first. Quite literally, the perfect dancing song, and one of my personal favorites. It was like he had done a background check on me to find out what I liked. To be honest, I wouldn't put it past his persistent personality.

"I'm a really awful dancer, Wyatt. Like, seriously. I don't want to embarrass you."

"The only way you could embarrass me is by forcing me to dance alone." He started to shimmy his way closer to me. I tried to back away, but he grabbed me before I could escape. He wrapped his hands around my waist, which started as playful and quickly transitioned to more intimate.

We swayed side to side for a handful of songs amongst the other dancing strangers. It was one of the strangest but most lovely sights I'd ever witnessed.

"You should give yourself more credit; you haven't even tripped once." His grip on my waist remained firm and warm. I felt way more comfortable than I thought I would, being this close to him.

"There's gotta be something." I gave him a sly look.

"What do you mean?"

"Something less than stellar about you. You know, planning all this..." I turned my head to scan the park. "Looking like that..." My eyes found his again. "What's the catch?"

"Well, Magnolia...I don't think there is a catch. And there shouldn't be, not when it comes to girls like you, at least. You feel like there has to be something wrong because your brain tricks you into thinking you're not worthy of things like this. But you are. You have no idea how worthy you are."

I couldn't stop smiling now. He had me wrapped around his damn finger with these eloquent speeches. I bet he didn't learn that in medical school.

"I'm the one not worthy...not worthy of that smile." he ran his thumb across my lip gently. "Not worthy of that laugh." I tried to hold it in, but a tiny giggle escaped. "And definitely not worthy of this."

He leaned in and kissed me softly. Once he realized that I was reciprocating, he became more passionate and less careful. His hands explored my body in a way that bordered on inappropriate for a public park, but I was too entangled to care.

He pulled away for a moment and looked me directly in the eyes. "So not worthy."

CHAPTER EIGHTEEN

It had been three weeks since my first date with Wyatt and things were going really well. We had finished off that first night with ice cream before I headed to Jen's house. I was so giddy in the car that I couldn't even turn on the radio. I just kept replaying the picnic and the dancing and the kiss in my head on repeat.

My dad was leaving for a 3-day golf trip with his friends so I invited Wyatt to spend the weekend with me. He jumped at the opportunity for some alone time. Luckily, the timing worked out, and he had two days off.

When he arrived, I gave him a very brief tour of my dad's drab condo. He set his stuff down and got comfortable in my room.

I still had some work to finish for Java June's Facebook marketing so he said he'd be fine just hanging out until I was done. Staying focused on my work while Wyatt lounged gorgeously on my bed was not easy, but I was trying to persevere for another hour. Then the weekend would be ours.

My phone rang in my pocket, and I pulled it out to see who was bothering me, us, this weekend. It was dad. Hopefully everything was okay because he normally didn't just call me to chat.

"Hey dad, what's up?"

"Mags, hey. Could you do me a favor real quick?"

"Sure."

"I forgot to bring the mail in before I left. I don't want it getting piled up; you know how Lillian gets."

For reference, Lillian is our mail lady who, I'm 99% certain, my father has a not-so-secret crush on. One time, Lillian mentioned that he had forgotten to put the flag up for an outgoing piece of mail, and I think my dad mistook it for flirting. So ever since, he'd been the most aggressively responsible mail customer ever. It was kind of cute actually.

"Yeah, for sure. I'll go grab it now. Anything else?"

"No, that's all. Have a fun weekend. Love you."

"I love you too, Dad."

He hung up, and I threw my phone in my bag on the floor. No more distractions. I had to get this done so that I could join the incredibly sexy doctor waiting for me in my bed. I turned to him.

"Hey, can I bother you for something super quick?"

His eyes perked up from the book he was reading.

"Anything."

"Can you just run out to the mailbox and grab the mail for me? My dad has a weird thing about leaving it in there for too long because he's secretly in love with our mail lady. Long story…"

"Say no more. Be right back." He hopped off the bed and left the room. Regardless of what he had said, I was definitely the not worthy one.

I turned back to my laptop, and my phone rang again. I swear this was the most action my phone had seen in a long time. It was probably just Jen calling to tell me about the kale salad she ate for lunch; she calls me all the time. I let the ring die out and forced myself back into focus mode. But it rang again and again so I finally grabbed it.

It was Roger. I don't think he'd ever called me in my life.

What the hell?

"Hi. What's up?"

"Maggie? It's Roger." His tone sounded different than usual.

"Is everything okay?"

"Maggie, it's your mom. I need help. She's um…she's not okay." Suddenly, I felt my heart beating wildly in my chest. Something wasn't right.

"What do you mean?" Suddenly, Wyatt walked back into my room holding a single envelope, not making any eye contact with me.

"Maggie, who's Nic Costelli?"

Oh no. Oh no no no no.

Not this. Not now.

I couldn't have this conversation right now. He finally looked up from the envelope and saw my concerned face still holding the phone up to my ear. He mouthed, "sorry" and sat on the edge of my bed. He placed the letter from Nic next to him like he was patiently waiting for me to explain myself.

"Roger, what happened?!" I pressed him again.

"She was out working in the garden, Maggie. I didn't hear her calling for me, but when I got up to get another beer, I checked on her and saw that she was on the ground. I immediately ran out to her but she's not responding. I tried CPR. I don't know what else to do. She won't wake up."

"Roger, what the fuck! You didn't call 911? She clearly needs an ambulance. Call them right now. I'll be there in a few." I slammed my laptop closed.

"It's my mom. She collapsed or something. My idiotic step-dad apparently doesn't know how to dial 3 simple numbers so I gotta go over there and try to help. I'm so sorry."

"What are you sorry for? Come on, let's go. I'll drive."

We hadn't even discussed meeting each other's parents yet, but he is a doctor after all. He confidently led me out of the room.

As I was closing my bedroom door, I looked at the letter still laying on my bed. Nic hadn't written in months, and, of course, a letter arrives today, of all days. I shut the door with a sigh and hurried out to Wyatt's car. I couldn't think about Nic or the letter or how I was going to explain all that to Wyatt yet. I pushed it out of my mind completely.

I gave Wyatt step-by-step directions to my mom's house; he was perfectly calm. He squeezed my hand reassuringly.

We pulled up to the house. There was an ambulance and a police car in the driveway, thank god. They were lifting my mom into the back on a stretcher. I jumped out of the still-moving car.

"Maggie!" Roger called out to me, but I ignored him and ran to the EMTs helping mom.

"What happened to her? Is she okay?"

One of them turned around to me slowly and gave me a piercing look. He didn't reply and hopped up into the vehicle.

"Hello? What the hell happened?"

Why was nobody answering me?

"Hey guys, what happened here?" Wyatt approached them from behind me. They seemed to be more inclined to talk to him for some reason. Probably because he's a man.

"Looks like a heart attack, but it's too soon to really tell. She's unresponsive, but we've got her on oxygen so she's stable for now. She's clearly been down a while, though. And in this heat..."

Wyatt's face dropped slightly.

"Thank you. Take her to Sparrow, please." The drivers nodded. "Maggie, you ride with her. I'll meet you there."

The entire ambulance ride was a blur. I watched my unconscious mother lay there, helpless, while the van hit pothole after pothole.

Fucking Michigan roads.

I held her hand even though it felt strange and unfamiliar.

When we arrived, they quickly took her away, and I met Roger and Wyatt in the lobby. They had driven together, which was both odd and somewhat endearing. I couldn't imagine what those two had to talk about on the drive here.

"Are you okay?" Wyatt embraced me in a long hug. Exactly what I needed.

"I am now." I squeezed him as tight as possible.

He kissed the top of my head and led me to the waiting room chairs where we sat for nearly 3 hours together, waiting for the doctor to give us an update. Wyatt just sat and held me without expecting a single thing.

I called my dad to tell him what had happened, and I could tell he was genuinely concerned for mom and for me. He even offered to leave his trip early to be with me, but I assured him that I was fine and had supportive company.

The doctor finally came out around 9pm and approached us somberly.

"Elizabeth's family?" We all stood up promptly.

"Yes. How is she?" Roger stepped slightly in front of us, eager to hear the update.

"Your wife did, in fact, suffer a heart attack. We proceeded with emergency surgery but, unfortunately, there were some complications. I'm so sorry, but your wife, Elizabeth, did not survive the surgery."

This was the first time I'd ever seen Roger cry. And it wasn't just a tear or two; he fully collapsed onto the floor and sobbed uncontrollably. The same man who broke up my parents' marriage. The same man who left my mother dying in the garden because he was too busy drinking beer and watching TV to hear her calling for him. The same man who I'll never be able to forgive for either of those things.

Although it took everything in me to do it, I crouched down next to him and held him as he wept. Regardless of my own personal issues with Roger, he did love my mother. And he was in unbearable pain right now.

My mom and I obviously didn't have a close relationship, but I still felt overwhelmingly sad when she passed away. Much sadder than I thought I would. Roger and I stayed there on the floor for what felt like hours.

When Wyatt brought me home from the hospital that night, I'm sure he could tell I was still in shock. He didn't pressure me to talk but still gave me all the affection I needed. He started cooking something for me in the kitchen while I went to take a shower and get rid of the hospital smell lingering on me.

I opened the door to my room and immediately saw Nic's letter still laying on my bed. I got incredibly frustrated by the sight of it for some reason and threw it in my desk drawer. I couldn't deal with Nic Costelli right now. And I definitely couldn't deal with Wyatt asking me questions about him.

Thankfully, when Wyatt returned to my room with a bowl of warm chicken noodle soup, he didn't ask about the letter. I was sure he'd bring it up in the future, but I was off the hook for now at least.

After I finished eating my soup, I climbed into bed with him. He held me, close and firm. It felt like he was literally holding me together. I closed my eyes tightly, breathing through the wave of emotions swirling inside me..Right as I was drifting into sleep, a tear fell from my eye.

Was it for my mom? Wyatt?

Nic?

Or maybe all of the above.

CHAPTER NINETEEN

Wyatt had been coming to see me every single day since mom had passed. I was so incredibly grateful. He seemed to be able to anticipate exactly what I needed at any time and then make it happen. Food? Check. Alone time? Check. I honestly don't know what I would've done without him during this time.

I brought boxes of mom's stuff from her house to my dad's because I couldn't stand sorting through them with Roger hovering over my shoulder. I started to fold her sweaters. I decided to place them in a box that would eventually be taken to a Goodwill for donation. Maybe Wyatt could do that. I smiled, thinking about how Wyatt had been offering to help me complete even the tiniest tasks, just to make sure I wasn't stressed about anything. And this was with him working 36-hour shifts like he was now.

I moved over to my desk to grab a sharpie marker, needing to label each box with its contents. I pulled the drawer out, and there it was.

Nic's letter staring me down. My stomach jumped into my

throat.

Why was I terrified to read it?

And why did I feel like my life was about to get really messy again?

Okay. I will read it. And then, I will move on from whatever it says. No matter what it says.

I slowly opened the letter:

Dear Magnolia,

I hope you're doing well. I know it's my fault for not keeping in touch, but I still miss you. I hope that's okay to say.

I'm sorry I haven't written for a while. Things have been crazy here. I've kind of been putting off writing to you because I really didn't want to say this in a letter, but I knew I wouldn't have the guts to say it over the phone.

I'm sure you know from Bel and Fran about us franchising Costelli Vineyards to Barcelona and Marseille. It's kind of amazing how quickly it's all been happening. Well, yesterday, Fran and Leone told me that they wanted me to be in charge of running the vineyard at home so they could focus on the other locations.

Can you believe it, Mags? I know it's going to be a ton of work, and that's partially why I'm writing this.

Mags, I want you to come back. No, I need you to come back. Come live here, and help me run the vineyard. You could be in charge of all the events, from initial client tours to weddings and everything in between. Come back and let's do this together. You know we make a good team.

And as much as I am trying to make this a business proposal, I'd be lying if I said I didn't want you to come back for my own selfish reasons as well. I said I'd wait for you, Mags, and, well, here I am.

Take all the time you need to decide. I've waited this long. A little longer won't kill me. I love you, Magnolia.

- Nic

The letter fell out of my hands, and I sunk down onto the floor beside it. I think time stopped completely. I could not look away from the floor for what felt like hours. I replayed the words in my head.

"Come back to me."

"I can't do this without you."

"We make a good team."

"I love you, Magnolia."

How dare he.

How fucking dare he drop this atomic bomb on me in a freaking letter. He doesn't write to me for months and then this?

I was finally able to pull my gaze up from the floor. I picked up the letter and folded it tightly. I stood up slowly and opened the drawer. I felt like I was in a trance. I couldn't think. I couldn't do anything. I placed the letter in the drawer.

As soon as I shut it, an uncontrollable flood of tears just poured out of me. I was crying so hard that I stumbled over a pile of clothes on my floor and landed face-down on the floor. I lay there, face-down, crying my eyes out for an hour.

I was in a new relationship with an amazing man who took such good care of me and may be the most generous person I'd ever met...meanwhile, I can't stop crying about stupid Nic Costelli and his stupid letter.

Once I was capable of pathetically peeling myself off the ground, I grabbed my keys and headed straight out the door without saying anything to my dad. There was one place I needed to be right now.

I drove down the familiar street to my childhood home. There were no cars in the driveway so I assumed the family wasn't home. Good. They didn't mind me coming over when they were here, but, obviously, it could be a little awkward: "Hey, I'm here to talk to my dead grandma through the tree again."

I sat with my back against the trunk. I hadn't sat out here in months. I'd been so busy with the new shop and Wyatt and my mom's passing. I needed her so much right now.

"Hi Gram," I whispered. With my finger, I traced my name that I had carved into the base when I was a kid.

"I'm so confused. You know Nic; I've told you about him before. The boy from the vineyard summer, not to be confused with his brother, August, also the boy from the vineyard summer. I know, it's getting hard for even me to keep up at this point. Don't judge." I rested my head back against the tree, trying to imagine I was leaning into her arms.

"Anyway, Nic did something super selfish and ridiculous and asked me to come back to the vineyard. Like, for good. To help him run it."

The fact that he just dropped that on me out of the blue is horrible. How the hell am I supposed to reply to that? I mean, does he even realize how much he's asking of me? How much I'd be giving up? Like Wyatt, for instance?"

There is no scenario in which I go back to that vineyard and Wyatt and I stay together.

"Gram...Nic is in my past. And he's confusing as hell. Wyatt feels like my future. He's kind and generous and stable. Frankly, he's perfect. Wyatt is a constant and Nic Costelli is the most uncertain uncertainty in this entire world."

My phone rang. It was Bel.

"Hey."

"Maggie! Hey! How's it going?"

"I'm...ok. How are you?"

"Well, it's funny you should ask. I'm actually at the airport."

"What airport? Where are you?"

"The Florence airport? Duh?"

"Oh. Where are you going?"

"Wait...are you joking? Mom said she told you."

"I haven't talked to Fran in a while...what's going on?"

"I could've sworn she told me that she called you to tell you, and Nic was sitting

right there when it happened. Why didn't he tell you?"

"Bel, can you please just tell me what the hell you're talking about right now?"

"Maggie... I got accepted to Michigan State. I was on the waitlist, and I was trying to keep it a secret from you because, honestly, I didn't think I would get in. They called me a week ago and said I was accepted. And Fran and Leone are letting me go there. So I've literally had a week to get ready to go. I get in tomorrow evening.

"What!? Oh my god. Bel, I can't believe this. And I can't believe Fran just 'forgot' to tell me. I'm so happy for you! And I'm so freaking excited that you're actually coming here."

"We're actually about to take off now so I gotta shut my phone off. But Maggie, I can't get into my dorm until Sunday. I was so eager to come, and I told mom the wrong date for my flight, and I couldn't fix it, and ugh. Do you think I could maybe stay with you tomorrow night? If it's not too much to ask?"

"And remember, I did willingly let you sleep in my room with me for like 6 months. You owe me," I missed Bel's sass so much.

"You better stay here. I'll text you my address, and you let me know when you land. Have a safe flight, Bel."

"I knew the guilt trip would work. See you soon!" She hung up.

I had plans with Wyatt tomorrow night, but I called him to tell him I'd be spending the night with a friend who was just getting into town unexpectedly. I didn't want to get into which friend, and he wasn't really the type to question me. He understood, of course, and told me he'd see me on Sunday.

I still couldn't believe I was about to see Bel in less than 24 hours. She was going to be in my actual house, here in the U.S. Not in our shared room on the vineyard.

I sat out under Gram's tree until it got dark, still trying to wrap my head around everything that had happened. I took a deep breath and closed my eyes for just a second. A few petals from the magnolia blooms fell on my head, and I opened my eyes to look up at them.

Thanks Gram. I love you too.

The next morning, I decided to run to the store to grab a few things for Bel's visit. We didn't keep many snacks in the house so I wanted to be sure to stock up before she arrived this afternoon. I also decided to grab a bottle of the "Magnolia" wine I last had on my first date with Wyatt. I figured Bel could do some explaining as to the reason my name was on one of her family's wines.

I lost track of time in the grocery store and didn't see that Bel had already texted me that she had landed and was getting into her Uber to my house. I rushed home as quickly as possible.

When I pulled into my driveway, I didn't see her anywhere. I figured she would've been here by now, but maybe the Uber was taking longer than expected. This was good. It would give me a few extra minutes to clean up my room and put the groceries away.

As I was walking to the garage, I heard a horn. I looked up and saw a car coming down the street, a hand waving out the window.

A Honda Civic pulled up, and Bel jumped out.

We both screamed and shared a long hug as the Uber driver took

Bel's luggage out of the trunk. We each rolled a suitcase as we walked inside. I introduced her to my dad, and then I motioned for her to follow me to my room. Once we got into my room, I shut the door, and she quickly tackled me onto the bed.

"I missed you so much. Not having a sister sucks!" We hugged tightly while laying on my bed.

"I missed you too, Bel. I don't share a room with my personal makeup and clothing stylist anymore."

She surveyed me up and down, noticing the paint stains on my jeans from working in the coffee shop.

"Yeah, I can tell." We both laughed. Bel always made me feel a lot prettier.

"So...what's new? Any new guys?"

"Well, once I finally broke free from the Costelli brother curse, I did meet someone pretty great."

"Should've taken my advice years ago."

"I know. But it all happened for a reason. Without all that, I wouldn't have met Wyatt."

"Wyatt...sounds very American. I like it. Tell me more." Bel propped herself on her elbow.

"He's a doctor, well, a resident, at a hospital near here."

"A DOCTOR?" Her eyes widened with intrigue.

"Yes, a doctor." I smiled and let her feel excited for me. It felt good.

"He works like 5 minutes from where you'll be going to school. Speaking of which, congrats on becoming a Spartan! I still can't believe nobody told me."

"Wow. That's a freaking step up from my stupid brothers, am I right?"

"Speaking of your stupid brothers, how's Nic?"

"How's Nic...hmm...all of the above."

"What do you mean?"

"He's ecstatic, he's terrified, he's excited, he's worried. He's everything. Of course, not all at once. Now that we know everything about your soap opera of a relationship with him, it kind of makes sense."

"Um...what? What do you mean you know everything about our relationship?"

"Well, he sort of broke down to mom a few nights before I left. I may or may not have been listening."

So typical of Bel to be snooping.

I desperately wanted to know what he'd said.

"He told her...something about a night in the jeep, something about the lake in the woods, a letter he was scared to send...I couldn't hear most of it, but...I knew it was about you."

I closed my eyes.

"Maggie, we've known since way back that you guys were meant to be together. He'd never looked at anyone the way he looked at you, not even Ellie. And you were just more yourself with him than with August. You seemed happy and not...stressed. I know I call my brothers idiots and stupid, but...Nic is a very good person. A very deep, loving, humble person. I see that now. And he's grown up a lot over the last couple years. You helped him get there."

"Why did nobody say anything? Why did you all just let me stay with August if you didn't think we were going to last?" You guys could've saved me a lot of heartache and pain if you would've just said something. I spent a year and a half trying to make the distance work with someone who...just wasn't capable of it."

"Maggie, you still don't get it?" She laughed softly to herself. "It wasn't our choice to make. You had to find out for yourself."

I couldn't believe what she was saying. Basically, they all thought August and I were totally wrong for each other, but nobody had the guts to tell me. Instead, everyone forced me to learn on my own that August and I were really never meant to be.

I get it. I was the one who was always preaching that we were "meant to be," us having met at Silk and then coincidently living with each other the next night. It all moved so fast, and it was exhilarating. From the minute I saw him in that towel, my mind was stubbornly made up. But now, knowing all that I do, would I have made a different choice?

I'd be lying if I said that since opening the letter, I hadn't thought about what it would be like if I went back and ran the vineyard with Nic. It sounds insane, but it also sounds like everything I've wanted but denied myself for years.

"He's been waiting for you this whole time. Just trust me when I say that you have constantly been at the forefront of his mind. If you take him up on his offer, you'll see that right away."

"Wait, what? You know about his offer? Did you read the letter?"

She refused to make eye contact with me and didn't answer my question.

"Bel, answer me."

"Okay fine! I saw him take a letter out to the mailbox one day, and I thought it was weird because he hadn't written to you or even talked about you in a while. I thought that was over. So when he came back inside I said I was going for a walk...but I went and looked at it. I'm sorry, Maggie! My nosiness is literally a disease. Please have your doctor boyfriend cure me of it."

"Shit. I was really hoping I could pretend that letter didn't exist. But now there were witnesses. You've complicated this completely, young lady."

I sighed as we lay there together on my bed. Bel reached her hand across the space in between us to grab mine. We stayed like this for a few minutes of silence as I reflected on what this all meant. We rolled over to face each other.

"Bel, what am I supposed to do?" There was a painfully loud silence occurring now between us. I watched her face very carefully. "I want to go back. I love the vineyard. I love Italy and the way I feel free there. And shit, Bel, I love him."

Tears began filling my tired eyes.

"I really think I always have. But Wyatt. This will break him. He doesn't deserve..."

She looked me directly in the eye, very subtly raising a single eyebrow. The fact that she said nothing said much more than her words possibly could have.

She finally spoke. "Maggie, I told you I came to college here in Michigan because of you. And, yeah, it would be a bummer if you weren't here to help guide me through these next four years, but it would really kill me to watch you settle for a life that I know isn't the one you truly want. I'm sure Wyatt is great…hell, he's a doctor…but he's not Nic. And you know that."

She squeezed my hand.

"Mags, I just want the best for my brother and my…sister." She rested her head on my shoulder. Hearing her call me Mags, just like Nic used to, made my heart swell up with a feeling I thought I'd never feel again.

We fell asleep just like that, and when I woke up the next morning, I felt an overwhelming wave of clarity. For the first time in a while, since staying in Italy all by myself with no idea of what was about to happen, I decided to take a chance on life's biggest uncertainty.

CHAPTER TWENTY

My mind is made up.

I think.

It better be because I bought my plane ticket late last night. I was thinking of Gram and Nic and felt a rush of spontaneity lying there next to Bel. I didn't put much thought into any of the goodbyes I had to face today. If I was going, I had to go right now so I didn't have time to chicken out. So, yeah...my flight leaves this afternoon.

I also hadn't called Nic to tell him I was taking him up on his offer. It had been a while since the letter came in the mail, and Nic could've changed his mind by now. I just kept putting it off, hoping I would get a sign that I'd made the right decision. I decided to start my goodbye tour with my dad. He would be the easiest to break the news to.

I sat down with him and tried to explain my logic, which wasn't truly all that logical. But I made it seem like I was mostly going for the business opportunity. It was a huge step up from my current job, it was in my dream field, you know, cookie-cutter excuses like that.

He didn't need to know everything about Nic right now.

He had a handful of logistical questions but seemed to be genuinely happy for me. I told him that I wasn't sure how long I'd be over there and that this whole plan could fail miserably, and he still said I was welcome to come home at any time.

One goodbye down, too many to go.

Next up, I called June and Levi. I offered to continue working on their digital marketing remotely, although, realistically, I was pretty sure I wouldn't have much time to devote to it. They were thrilled to keep me on in any capacity. June took the phone from Levi at the end and told me she thought I was making the right decision.

"Love may be patient, but it's still relentless. Go, Maggie. Follow your heart, wherever it leads." I will carry that message with me forever; she always knew the right thing to say.

I decided to be super brief in my explanation to Bec and Jen. I gave them the bare minimum details and promised them I would call once I got to Italy. It was probably shitty of me to be so abrupt, but I just didn't have time. And they both responded exactly the way I knew they would: Bec freaking out and peppering me with really good questions; and Jen being sweet and starry-eyed and wishing me well.

I just kept telling myself I would figure all this out once I got there and figured out if Nic even wanted me to be there still.

Now I had to face Wyatt. I'd been feeling nauseated about this confrontation ever since I woke up.

He was meeting me for coffee this morning. I spent the entire drive over in the Uber planning out what to say to the perfect man whose heart I was inexplicably about to shatter. There was simply no good way to say, "Hey, I'm breaking up with you to go live on a vineyard in Italy with my ex-boyfriend's brother who I've been secretly in love with for years."

Shit. It sounded way worse than I thought.

Wyatt and I had only been dating for a month so this shouldn't have felt like such a big deal, but our relationship had gotten serious incredibly quickly. He was also one of the kindest, most deeply caring people I'd ever met. I wished more than anything that there was a way for me and him to remain friends after this, but I knew that was a selfish thought. I couldn't have both, I never could.

I walked into the cafe and saw Wyatt waiting for me at a table with two coffees placed in front of him. His smile lit up when his eyes met mine. At that moment, I almost changed my mind. Seeing him sitting there, eagerly waiting to spend time with me and knowing I was about to crush his heart, I didn't think I could do it. Maybe this was all a mistake.

I continued to walk toward him, trying to slow my breathing so he wouldn't be immediately suspicious. Once I neared the table, he stood and wrapped an arm around my back, kissing me softly on my cheek. It was too late. I had to commit to my decision now. I tried to remember Levi's words in my head. Love is relentless.

"Hello, beautiful." He pulled the chair out for me. He's that guy. The type that pulls the goddamn chair out for me.

"Hi. Thanks for meeting me." This came out more businesslike than I had planned.

"Of course...Although, I must admit this is scaring me a bit. Is everything okay?"

Here goes nothing. Time to rip the bandaid off.

"Wyatt…"

Before I could even say anything, his face fell, and he wouldn't look at me. He knew.

"Wyatt, look at me."

"It's alright, Magnolia. You don't have to say it. I can hear it in your voice." He didn't sound angry, just hurt and disappointed.

"You're breaking up with me." He stated this bluntly, without hesitation.

A long pause lingered in the air between us. I was staring down at the table. Even amidst the busyness of the cafe at this hour, the silence was excruciating.

"Is this about that letter you got in the mail? From that Nic guy?"

"We haven't exactly had the past relationships conversation yet. But that's no excuse. I should've told you about Nic and me sooner."

I took a long, slow inhale.

"I told you that I worked on a vineyard near Florence, but I didn't tell you about the family. They had three kids. Two boys and a girl, August, Nic and Bel. Long story short, I ended up dating August that summer. We tried to make it work after I left, but the distance was too much. Nic and I were really close friends, until he told me he loved me the night before I left. It was craziness, truly. Talking about it now sounds like a rom-com, but, at the time, it was real and a huge chapter in my life. Anyway, in the letter, Nic basically asked me to come back to the vineyard and…work and live there…full time. He's taking it over from his parents, and he wants

WHERE THE MAGNOLIA TREES BLOOM

to do like a partnership with me."

"Okay, so where in that story was the part where you said that you love Nic back?" Shockingly, he still didn't seem angry. "I saw the way you reacted when I brought in that letter from the mailbox. You looked like you had seen a ghost."

"Wyatt…Nic and I haven't spoken in a while. Definitely not since I met you. When he wrote to me and, out of the blue, asked such a massive question, I was completely thrown off guard. It's not like I was doing anything behind your back. I was basically just trying to process what he'd said in the letter…and make a decision."

"I'm not accusing you of doing anything behind my back. I just don't want you to sugarcoat any of this for me." He grabbed my hand across the table which took me by complete surprise.

"Do you love him?"

My gaze moved down to the table between us then back up to meet his.

"I think I do," I whispered.

"Don't diminish your feelings for my sake, to soothe my wounded ego. I can take it. You're in love with someone else, and I can take it. I'll be ok. Sure, it fucking sucks, but I would never be mad at you for simply feeling what I feel for you, for someone else. I know how powerful it can be."

Is he saying he loves me?

How do I leave this cafe if that's what he's saying?

I squeezed his hand tightly.

"Wyatt, you have no idea how sorry I am for all of this."

"Don't apologize."

241

I could see the sadness lingering in the corners of his smile. The fact that he was taking this so well didn't really surprise me all that much. He'd been nothing but caring and generous and wonderful this past month. Which only made me feel ten times worse for doing this. It would've been much easier if he'd gotten angry and thrown a fit, called me a bunch of names, and then stormed out.

I smiled back at him.

"Wyatt..."

He cut me off again.

"Go, Magnolia."

I stared at him.

"I'm serious. Go. Life's too short. Believe me, I know. Now go get on that damn plane."

Wiping away my tears, I stood up, heading for the door before I changed my mind. As I pushed the door slightly open, I paused, wanting to look back at him, but then re-routed myself.

All I could hear in my head as I made my way out of the cafe was Gram's voice.

"Move forward, Magnolia. You are ready for this."

CHAPTER TWENTY-ONE

It was really hard for me to imagine Nic running the entire vineyard himself. I'm sure Fran and Leone trained him well, and he was naturally super smart, but he didn't exactly have a Type-A personality. He was much more like Leone than Fran. He preferred quiet over mindless small-talk, like me, and that was just one of the things I loved about him.

Love.

I'm still not used to allowing myself to associate that word with Nic. In just a few hours, I would be saying the words to him in person. My heart was racing just thinking about it.

I gulped down the $9.50 mimosa I'd splurged on and leaned my head against the window, trying for a moment to locate the ground thousands of feet below us. I quickly became dizzy and decided to shut my eyes. My mind wandered to the days working on the vineyard, sitting out by the lake, watching the sunrise, and Nic and I sitting together quietly. There had been so many instances where he and I had just sat, perfectly silent, embracing the stillness and beauty around us. It was always a nice breather from August's constant desire to discuss "things."

Not all the memories were pure and simple and pleasant like those, however. I still thought all the time about the night in the Jeep with Nic. I wasn't sure if I'd fully forgiven myself for kissing him. I thought about Nic and August's fight. I thought about the accident in the Jeep. I thought about the way Nic had behaved toward me when I first got to the vineyard. Those memories still hurt. But they struck me differently now. It seems to me now that life puts obstacles, conflicts, in our path to get our attention when something's not right, and it's our job to figure out what the conflicts are trying to tell us. At least, that's what makes sense to me at this point.

While I walked through the Florence Airport lobby to grab a taxi outside, I couldn't help but remember that day I'd stood right there arguing with Bec and Jen about my decision to stay in Italy.

I laughed to myself. God, how stupid I must've sounded trying to justify that completely irresponsible choice. It couldn't be explained. It was purely a gut decision.

I refused to believe in fate. I hated when people tried to rationalize good things happening to them by believing in some imaginary and invisible power out of our control. We are the only people who can control what happens to us. And that day, two years ago, in this same place, I decided to take a chance. And that decision alone is what changed my life.

Fate doesn't find you; you create it.

I texted Bel a selfie of me in the airport with the message "here goes nothing" and a fingers crossed emoji.

I absolutely hated talking to taxi drivers, and every time I got into one I hoped and prayed that they wouldn't like talking much either. This one, of course, decided to tell me his entire life story, with the thickest Italian accent I'd ever heard.

I nodded, probably too many times, just to show him I was "listening," but I couldn't think about anything other than what I was about to do. I loved spontaneous adventures. Hell, I said yes to living on a vineyard with a complete stranger I'd spoken to for 5 minutes in the midst of a worldwide pandemic. But I was truly terrified -- even more terrified than I'd been heading to the vineyard that first time.

After about an hour and a half in the car, the driver stopped at the end of the driveway. He mumbled something about how his tires had already endured enough, and he wanted to see if my "little legs" could manage the driveway on my own. I laughed, understanding him just enough to know what to do.

"Thank you sir!" I called after him, but he was already driving away, probably still telling the story of his eldest daughter's birth out loud to himself.

I took a deep breath and turned to face the house, foolishly hoping I wouldn't see anyone before I had a chance to get inside and clean up a bit. I looked like hell, even though I tried to do my makeup in the bathroom on the plane.

This was one of those rare instances I felt that makeup might be necessary, I wanted to at least look good if I was about to meet the woman Nic had fallen in love with and invited to help run the vineyard in my place.

Using humor as a coping mechanism often helped tremendously in situations like this. Mainly because the things I worried about usually didn't happen.

Usually.

This situation, of course, was the one where my worst fear seemed scarily accurate.

As I got closer to the house, I saw a tall blonde woman standing in the kitchen with her back towards the window. She was talking on the phone, flipping the ends of her hair between her fingers.

There she was.

Probably sipping her morning coffee that Nic had brewed for her before heading into town, leaving her at home to handle the calls that needed to be made this morning. I was too late, and this was about to be a very awkward situation. But, hey, I've definitely had practice with those. Surely I couldn't tell this woman that I had flown halfway around the world to confess my love for her boyfriend.

I braced myself and headed toward the side door, feeling the familiarity as if no time had passed at all.

Do I knock?

Hell, no. I probably lived here longer than this bitch has.

The familiarity of the knob turning in my hand was like I was just heading in from another day working.

As I entered, the woman turned around, still holding the phone to her ear. She looked confused to see me, but only for a moment. Her face quickly transitioned from curious to intrigued.

Hold on. I think I know this woman. How do I know her?

She wrapped up the phone call to be able to speak to the

stranger standing in what was apparently now her kitchen.

"Babe, let me call you back. I have a...visitor...here in the kitchen. Just give me a few. Love you." She hung up and set the phone on the counter.

Of course, she calls him babe.

I wonder what he calls her.

Who the hell is this and why does she look so familiar?

"You're...you're Maggie, right?" Still frustrated that I couldn't figure out how I knew this woman, I reached my hand out in an attempt to be cordial.

"Hi. Yeah, I'm Maggie. I used to live here for a bit...it's a funny story...I was studying abroad and then..." I realized I was literally stuttering.

"Yeah, I know. We've met." She cut me off. "When you were with Bel in Montaione. I'm Lucy. It's nice to see you again." She reached out. As I went to shake her perfectly manicured hand, I was nearly blinded by the obscenely large diamond shining brightly on her ring finger.

I knew it.

Lucy. The Lucy that ditched August at prom for Nic. The Lucy that must've been in love with Nic since then and had finally made her move. The Lucy that was marrying Nic.

MY Nic.

How the hell did I not see this coming? I should've been quicker putting that together, but her hair was chopped, and she was dressed more like a fiancé. I couldn't speak.

Engaged? Seriously?

I didn't reply to the letter for a few weeks, and he goes and gets freaking engaged? And to this bimbo? My breathing started to pick up speed as I felt the panic creeping up. I was going to have to make up some elaborate lie as to why the hell I was here.

"Sorry, I didn't recognize you with…with the haircut. It looks great." I offered her a smile, when all I really wanted to do was roll my eyes.

"Thank you, Maggie." She paused. "My goodness, I'm being such a terrible host. Can I get you something to drink? Some coffee? You must be tired from your…travels."

Of course she was playing this role. And the way she said travels was obnoxiously condescending. There were no way she could actually know why I'm here. So no, Lucy, I don't want your fucking coffee. I don't want your hospitality. And I sure as hell don't want you here.

"Sure, coffee sounds good." I faked another smile.

She pulled out a baby blue mug from the cupboard that had "New Jersey" in cursive letters on it. I've drunk out of that mug countless times, but watching her hands reach for it so confidently, like she owned the place, made me want to smash it into a million tiny pieces.

She poured the coffee and gestured to me to come join her at the kitchen table. I hoped this woman did not expect me to sit and chit-chat about the only thing we had in common. The man I came here to confess my love for.

I sat down next to her and took a long sip of the coffee as I wrapped my hands around the warmth of the familiar mug. I glanced at her ring again.

"So, Maggie. What brings you back to the great Costelli vineyard?"

Here we go. My acting skills are ready to shine.

"I'm here to visit Fran!" I said enthusiastically. "She bought me a flight to thank me for helping get Bel settled into school. It was really way too generous, but that's how Fran rolls."

I watched her eyes survey my every move. Not even the tiniest trace of a smile hid behind her stoically flawless face. She was onto me. I could feel it.

"Oh, how sweet is that. Typical Fran." She propped her chin up onto her hands as she leaned in closer to me. "But…Fran isn't here, Maggie. She's with Leone visiting the property in Barcelona. They won't be back for another day or two. I'm sure she must've mentioned that when inviting you to come here, right?" The patronizing bullshit in her voice was nauseating.

But she got me there. I didn't even think to see if Fran was here or not.

"Right. I obviously knew that. But I got off work a few days earlier than I anticipated and Fran said I could just come whenever. So I figured what's the harm in an extended vacation. Was hoping to maybe catch one of the boys if they were around."

"Sure, that makes sense. Nic is out there somewhere. He left early this morning, and he hasn't come back since. He's such a hard worker, you know…great with his hands."

I winced at the thought of her knowing anything about what his hands are capable of. Was she trying to torture me on purpose?

"That's okay. I can just wait here or up in Bel's room for him to get back. Thanks, Lucy…for the coffee." I stood up and walked my empty mug to the sink.

"You know…" She raised her eyebrows at me. "He's been waiting. Never stops talking about you. Maggie this, Maggie that. And trees. Magnolia trees. He's so damn obsessed with them these days."

I felt a flutter in my stomach when I heard that he talked about me and Gram's tree. And the lack of jealousy in her voice led me to believe she was somehow okay with him waiting for me to come back.

I was starting to get really confused.

What type of weird open relationship did these two have going on where it was okay for your fiancé to never stop talking about someone from their past? But then again, maybe Lucy didn't know about our past. Maybe she just thought we were really close friends and she was okay with it because it made him happy.

She stood up and made her way over to me still standing at the sink, gliding effortlessly as her white sandals clicked loudly across the floor. She was standing close to me now. Way too close for my liking.

"He's going to be really, really glad you're here. But if you…if you break his heart again…you're going to be dealing with me this time. Okay? Just don't hurt him, please."

She was looking deep into my soul which scared the shit out of me. I feared breaking her gaze would have its own set of consequences so I just nodded slowly in agreement.

The side door swung open dramatically. "Who's hurting who?"

I assumed it was Nic returning from the vineyard for lunch. But I was quite wrong.

August stood there, slowly pushing his black sunglasses up onto his head.

His face froze as he made eye contact with me.

Speechless...for the first time in his life?

I couldn't really tell what he was feeling but, overall, he didn't look thrilled to see me standing in his kitchen. It had been almost a year since we had spoken.

I hated to admit it, but he looked absolutely amazing. London had been good to him. He had put on a little weight, but it actually suited him. His hair was even longer than before, and he had a goatee. He definitely looked the part of a budding filmmaker.

I had thought that the next time I saw him, I would feel some sadness or grief about our relationship ending, but, standing here now, I felt surprisingly okay.

"Maggie...what are you doing here?" The concern in his voice was endearing.

"She's here for Nic, babe." Lucy immediately interjected from behind me.

Babe? Did she just call August "babe"?

Jesus, is this a freaky threesome situation? My brain hurts.

"What's going on? Why are you home and not in London?" I took a step toward August, ignoring Lucy's comment completely. I didn't know much about his life post-graduation and post-breakup, but I did know from my brief conversations with Fran that he was still living in London and working for a small production company.

"I'm just home for the weekend. Lucy and I got in last night. We, uh, have some news we wanted to share with mom and dad when they get back from Barcelona tomorrow."

I'm such a freaking idiot.

Lucy isn't Nic's fiancé. She's August's. I think the shock was showing unintentionally on my face. Lucy stepped in between us.

"I'm going to let you two talk for a bit. I'll be right outside." She kissed August's cheek which, surprisingly, made me happy. Seeing him with someone who obviously cared for him reassured me that he would be okay when he found out why I was really here.

When Lucy exited the kitchen, August took a step closer to me leaving a few feet between us. His head was lowered.

"I was going to call you, Maggie. It just all happened much more quickly than I could've anticipated. When I started my new job, Lucy messaged me on Facebook telling me she was moving to London for her job. She wanted to have a friend in the area, and she knew I lived there. I was hesitant because we literally hadn't spoken since prom, and you know how poorly that ended. But...we started hanging out, just as friends at first, but when you and I officially called it quits, it sort of transitioned into something more. Something unexpected."

The intercom.

That was Lucy's voice on the damn intercom.

It took every ounce of my strength to not tell him about my trip to London to see him. I wanted him to know how much hearing her voice hurt me. How long it took me to get over that and find peace with our breakup. But that would do neither of us any good to get into those details right now.

"Wow. That's sort of...crazy. How that all worked out, with you being prom dates and all." I smiled at him, which I could tell eased his anxiety; he smiled right back.

"Trust me, she's had to make up for the prom thing. Definitely not the same Lucy as when we were kids. I know I probably didn't give you a very flattering first impression of her. The whole marriage thing came up really quickly; we both just sort of knew. We thought why wait? I know it probably seems insane to you. I hope you're not upset. I should've told you sooner."

Before he could say anything else, I reached out and grabbed him for a long and steady hug. It felt warm and comfortable and familiar.

I pulled away and looked up at him.

"So you're not upset?"

"August, I'm really happy for you. She's beautiful, and I can tell she loves you very much. I just can't believe... you're engaged."

"It's all pretty crazy to me still, but thank you, Maggie." He smiled softly. "Well, now that you know why I'm here, I think we should talk about why you are."

I was now making uncomfortable eye contact with the coffee maker.

"Does he even know you're here?"

My eyes jumped to August's.

He already knew.

We stared at each other

Finally, I spoke. "No...I haven't talked to him about it. But when Bel got to Michigan a few days ago, she stayed the night with me when she couldn't get into the dorm yet. She basically persuaded me to come. You know Bel, she's into those hopeless romantic movies...but it's stupid. I shouldn't have come all the way here without saying something to him first."

"It's not stupid, Maggie. You know he's going to be so incredibly excited to see you. Are you here...for good? Or are you just visiting?"

"I don't really know, to be honest. Maybe for good? If he still wants me to, you know."

"I'm sure he does. But you should go talk to him yourself. He's probably out in the vines somewhere. He told me this morning at breakfast that he had some incredible new project he was excited about out there."

"Thank you, August. I really am happy for you," I whispered into his ear as I hugged him again.

"I'm happy for you too Maggie, and I'm glad we both ended up where we were meant to be." He was holding me longer than the first hug. "And who we were meant to be with."

It felt like everything leading up to this moment finally made sense, and I suddenly had a huge surge of courage. I pulled away from the hug, gave him one last look, and headed out the door.

When I passed Lucy, who was sitting on a lawn chair, we shared a brief glance before she winked at me. Maybe she's not that bad after all. And I strictly mean maybe.

I could feel my worries start to flood away as I headed out into the vineyard searching for Nic. A surge of excitement rushed through me as I realized what was about to happen. *Finally.*

I searched the first few rows of vines and didn't see him. Finally, I reached a huge plot of land that had recently been cleared and had rows of young trees that looked freshly planted. Was this the project August was talking about?

I started walking towards the trees when my foot caught something hard in the grass. I nearly fell flat on my face. I looked down and saw a wooden sign that had been pushed deep down into the dirt. I stepped back to get a better look at it.

"Maggie's Magnolias," the sign read in crisp, white paint.

I read the sign again, and again, and yet again, before looking up at the endless rows of trees directly in front of me. Back down at the sign. Back up at the trees.

I looked a little closer and realized these were all young magnolia trees that hadn't bloomed yet. I stood there, remembering how beautiful it was when the magnolia tree we'd planted in the yard at home had its first bloom. I couldn't imagine what an entire field of them would look like.

I stood there in complete disbelief, when I heard someone approach behind me.

"Mags?"

I quickly turned around and saw Nic standing there. He looked like he hadn't shaved in a few days. His hair was a complete mess, sticking out at all angles from underneath a dirty baseball hat.

"Hi." That was all I could get out.

"Hi," he said, smiling. He took a step towards me. "I see you've found your trees. They've been quite the project, let me tell you."

"My trees?"

"Didn't you read the sign?" He motioned toward the ground.

"Yeah, but...Nic...You planted all of these...for me? Why?"

He laughed like he knew I would say that.

"Well...I just wanted it to feel a little more like home for you when you finally decided to take me up on my offer. And I knew, when you did come, you'd miss Gram's tree back home, so I figured why not plant a hundred or so just to be safe."

I could feel the tears coming.

"How did you know I'd come?"

"Because you're smart -- too smart for your own good. And I knew you'd figure it out eventually. I told you I'd wait, didn't I?"

"Figure what out?" Now I was just playing dumb, but I really liked hearing him talk. I'd missed his voice so much.

He took a step closer.

"You know how being under your Gram's tree makes you feel the most at home? It's the place where you're the safest and able to be completely yourself with no judgement or stress."

I nodded slowly.

"...That's exactly how you make me feel, Maggie. Wherever I am with you, no matter what we're doing, it always feels like home. Like nobody's going to judge me or look at me like the broken kid. You make me feel safe to be me, pain and all. And I guess I just wanted to repay you for that by giving you a place that's all yours, where you can come at any time and hopefully feel close to Gram."

He grew closer, leaving barely a few inches between us.

"You think she would've liked them?" I stood there speechless, not even trying to stop the tears as I nodded.

"What finally made you decide to come?"

"Bel, believe it or not. And another friend. And Gram."

I wiped my eyes with my sleeve. "They helped me build up my courage. And they...helped me tell myself the truth. A truth I've been resisting for a while now."

"What truth was that?" He smirked. "I'm better looking than my brother after all?"

I gave him a playful nudge in the chest and rolled my eyes.

He laughed and then took a slow deep breath. "You want to hear my truth, Mags?"

I nervously played with the ring on my thumb while he grew closer, leaving barely a few inches between us.

"My truth is that I am, and have been, overwhelmingly in love with a girl who is quite literally the clumsiest person I've ever met. A girl who claims to be good at directions, but misses that left turn to Elliott's every single time."

I burst out laughing and shrugged in agreement.

He took my hands and pulled me closer. "A girl who finds beauty in things that most people find ordinary, like lakes and..." he paused to look out behind me, "trees."

"A girl who loves to be alone. Who feels most content in silence. But for some reason still allows me, the temperamental jerk, to intrude on that solitude. A girl whose nose scrunches when she laughs."

I couldn't stop smiling.

"But I think the thing I love most about this girl...is how much she cares about people. There's not a selfish bone in her body. She'd drop anything to help someone that needed it, even when that someone is a drunk idiot that needs to be rescued from a party."

Our noses were now almost touching; I could feel his warm breath brushing against my cheeks.

"Magnolia…"

"Nic, I love you."

God, that felt good.

Nic closed his eyes momentarily, and a single tear rolled down his cheek. "I love you, Magnolia."

Our words lingered in the thick air between us for a split-second before he was kissing me passionately…making up for lost time and lost moments. We kissed and allowed our hands to explore each other's trembling bodies, finally, with nothing to hide.

He pulled away slowly after a few minutes. "I'll plant a thousand more trees if it means you'll stay here with me. For good."

I looked back at the vast field of my trees, ready to blossom.

"I would've stayed if you hadn't planted even a single tree."

We hugged tightly; he lifted me off the ground and spun me around, then set me down gently. I never wanted this moment to end.

I rested my head on his chest, while we looked out over the Magnolia trees, the house and barns in the distance.

"Feels good to be home," I whispered.

The End

AUTHOR'S NOTE

Dear Reader,

I cannot thank you enough, from the bottom of my heart, for reading my book. Much like Magnolia's journey, writing this was an adventure for me as well. One that was filled with sleepless nights worrying about typos and too many spilled coffees on the early rough drafts which I (foolishly) tried to edit by hand.

Without you taking the time to read it, that journey would've ended with this manuscript sitting in my drafts forever. I hope you enjoyed the characters and story as much as I have this past year.

If I could just ask one more favor before you go…I'd love to hear your thoughts and reactions to the book. Any comment is a helpful one. If you would kindly please leave a review on Amazon, I would greatly appreciate it!

Until next time,

Emily Comos